"THIS IS THE FIRST THING
THAT HAS TO GO. I LIKE MY WOMAN'S HAIR
DONE IN A MORE SOPHISTICATED STYLE."

Jacinda slipped the band off her ponytail and shook it.
His eyes moved appreciatively over the generous froth of
hair. "Next the sweater will have to go." He reached down
to pull it over her head.

Jacinda captured his hands in hers, laughing. "This is
as far as you go."

"Jacinda," he whispered. "Maybe the solution to our
clothes problems is for both of us to take them off. I'll go
first if you'd like."

She was tempted. In the privacy of her bedroom all the
differences between them wouldn't matter. But of course
they did. Slowly, regretfully, she drew back. "No, we'd
probably better go now."

The spirit was willing, but when his mouth captured
hers in a languorous, intoxicating kiss, she responded instantly and eagerly. Between them arced an electrifying
sensation that fanned embers of passion. Their mouths
clung as if each depended on the other for their life's
breath.

A CANDLELIGHT ECSTASY ROMANCE ®

WHEN
OPPOSITES
ATTRACT

Candice Adams

A CANDLELIGHT ECSTASY ROMANCE ®

Published by
Dell Publishing Co., Inc.
1 Dag Hammarskjold Plaza
New York, New York 10017

ISBN: 0–440–19674–4

Printed in the United States of America
First printing—April 1984

To Tom and Sharon,
with affection

To Our Readers:

We have been delighted with your enthusiastic response to Candlelight Ecstasy Romances®, and we thank you for the interest you have shown in this exciting series.

In the upcoming months we will continue to present the distinctive sensuous love stories you have come to expect only from Ecstasy. We look forward to bringing you many more books from your favorite authors and also the very finest work from new authors of contemporary romantic fiction.

As always, we are striving to present the unique, absorbing love stories that you enjoy most—books that are more than ordinary romance.

Your suggestions and comments are always welcome. Please write to us at the address below.

Sincerely,

The Editors
Candlelight Romances
1 Dag Hammarskjold Plaza
New York, New York 10017

CHAPTER ONE

"Arkansas?" Jacinda stared blankly at the man standing inside her office door.

"Yes." Jim Peters grinned. "I see the name doesn't seem to ring a bell to you. It's one of the fifty states."

She was already shaking her head, and the cascade of dark curls bounced back and forth. It was out of the question, even if it was only for six months. "I'm sorry, Jim, but I don't think so."

He advanced into the room, serious now. "Jacinda. I know it's a lot to ask. Hell, there's probably not one person in all of New York City who wants to go there. But we're in a bind since Dave Mitchell had a heart attack. Someone's got to take over and you're good at this sort of thing."

"I'm not going, Jim, and that's final."

After a week in Fayetteville, Arkansas, Jacinda was more convinced than ever that she had made a mistake in letting Jim talk her into coming. She missed New York already, and it would be six long months before she could return. The one bright spot so far was that she had met Philip, a handsome man with brown hair and blue eyes who was also a transplant from the East Coast and as anxious to return as she. Philip taught at the University of Arkansas but was trying desperately to find a position in the East. He and Jim Peters were good friends—it was Jim who had arranged their meeting.

Jacinda was thinking about him, and New York, as she sat in her office at the Ozark Power Company. It was housed in a new building with smoked glass in the windows, grasscloth on the walls, and rubber plants backed into the corners. A great deal of work had accumulated since Dave Mitchell, the electrical engineer she was replacing, had his heart attack.

Fingering the tie of her cinnamon silk blouse, Jacinda scanned the proposal she had just finished reading. It was simply worded and the accompanying drawings were also straightforward. The owner of a small rock quarry was requesting a permit to sell surplus electricity to the power company. Although she had occasionally reviewed such requests in New York, they had usually been from large companies, not individuals.

Not that it made any difference who produced the electricity; the power companies were obligated by law to buy surplus kilowatts. She was familiar with plans to incorporate solar, water, and wind energy into the power company's lines. What she had not seen before was a plan such as this one.

10

The proposal in front of her was from one Eric Fortner. Granted, it was neatly written and the person who had drawn the blueprints seemed to have a basic understanding of electrical engineering. But there was one large problem. She didn't think Eric Fortner's plans to use the conveyor from his quarry to generate electricity would work.

"What do you think of Eric's plan?"

Jacinda looked up as Lann Weston stepped into the room. He was a short, heavily built man with thick black hair and a shy smile. She liked him. After only a week she was sure they were going to work well together. Although Lann was her boss, he was a mechanical engineer by training and seemed content to let her have free rein on electrical matters while he confined himself to office management.

"I've looked it over. I'm afraid it won't work."

He seemed disappointed as he ran stubby fingers through his hair. "Oh?"

"No. The electricity produced would come in uneven surges. It'd be too risky to put this system on line and chance shorting out our equipment. I'll write a memo explaining that to Mr. Fortner." Briskly she began rolling up the blueprint. Now that this was disposed of, she could get on with other work.

"Er, Jacinda . . ."

She glanced up. "Yes?"

"I wonder if it'd be possible for Eric to come in and talk to you. I know he's really hoping to get this off the ground, and he's put a lot of time into it.

11

Maybe there's something you could suggest to make his plan work," Lann concluded hopefully.

Jacinda brushed back her mahogany curls. Immediately they returned to their original position framing her oval face. "I don't know . . ." she began doubtfully.

"Just talk to him," Lann coaxed.

"Of course." Lann was, after all, her boss.

He beamed at her. "That's a girl! I'll call him now. I imagine he can drive right in."

It was less than a half hour later when Jacinda looked up to see a tall, blond-haired man entering her office. He was wearing navy slacks, a light blue shirt, and a navy tie. His deep, permanent tan suggested he spent a good deal of his time outdoors. Lann was beside him, looking even more squat next to the rangy leanness of his companion.

"Jacinda, this is Eric Fortner."

As Eric approached her desk, he straightened the knot of his tie. Something about the way he wore his clothes suggested they weren't his usual attire. Her suspicion was confirmed when she noticed the faint fold lines on his shirt, evidence that it had recently emerged from its package. No doubt the shirt and the trousers were his "best" clothes, and he had put them on to come to her office.

"How do you do, Mr. Fortner?" She extended her hand and found it enveloped in a firm, warm grasp.

"Fine, thanks. Pleased to meet you." He dropped the ends of his words and put the accent in odd places. Jacinda had heard a good deal of the Arkansas dialect in the last week. Some of it was a little jarring, but on his lips the words sounded almost lyrical.

"Sit down, please." He sat in the chair she'd indicated and stuck his hands into his pockets, then withdrew them and laid them on his knees, looking very ill at ease.

She found his awkwardness rather touching. Eric Fortner was a good-looking man, even if he wasn't particularly polished. Of course, he was quite different from Philip, who had known the correct wine to order with their dinner last night and who handled himself with such finesse.

Lann beamed happily. "I'll just let you two talk. Call me if you need anything." He closed the door behind him, leaving them alone.

Jacinda settled back in her brown leather chair. She didn't want to keep Eric Fortner in suspense, so she went directly to business. "I've reviewed your proposal, Mr. Fortner. I understand why you want to use the conveyor in your quarry to generate electricity. As you may be aware, Ozark Power is obligated to buy any surplus electricity produced by an individual. The problem is, we can only allow systems that are compatible to our own to tap into ours."

She paused and tilted her head curiously to the side. Eric Fortner didn't seem to be listening. Instead, he was glancing around the room, looking first up toward the ceiling, then down at the floor. In fact, he appeared completely absorbed in his study of her office. Purposefully, she cleared her throat. "Mr. Fortner."

Cocoa brown eyes came to rest on her. "Yes?"

"Did you understand what I said?"

"Not entirely." His apologetic smile revealed a row of even teeth and a roguish dimple in one cheek.

He was a nice package to be so dense. Jacinda repressed a sigh and began again, more simply. "You see, Mr. Fortner, we have this large plant that makes electricity—" She broke off. Once again, she seemed to have lost his attention. "I'll be frank—"

"Then I'll be Eric." The brown eyes rested on her with an unmistakable teasing glint.

Was he for real? She was used to dealing with crisp, professional men, but Eric obviously wasn't one of those. Neither did he seem to be versed in the complexities of the power company. As she sat looking at him and trying to decide how to proceed, it was impossible not to notice how attractive he was. Physically, at least, he was perfect. His hair was cut casually and looked natural—not like the coiffed, blow-dried styles so many men wore and that made them seem somehow vain. There was no vanity here, but she was beginning to catch a glimpse of a raw confidence she had not at first expected of him.

"May I say something?" he asked courteously.

Instantly her thoughts returned to business. "Please do."

He seemed more at ease as he rested a long arm on one knee and used the other to pluck a speck of lint from his navy trousers. "I understand that you're saying my plan won't work." He grinned disarmingly and the dimple reappeared. "But you're wrong. It's an easy mistake to make since what we're talking about is a new frontier in electricity."

Jacinda felt a spark of indignation. Was the man questioning her knowledge of electrical engineering? She lifted her chin proudly. "I agree that what you propose is on the edges of technology and this isn't a precise science. However, skilled electrical engineers are constantly experimenting to learn more about the field." She hoped he understood her tactful use of the word *skilled*. She didn't want to hurt his feelings, but it seemed plain he was out of his element. However appealing his smile might be, and however pleasant she might find the cadence of his speech, she had a job to do. And that meant rejecting his proposal.

"My plan will work." Eric spoke slowly, clearly, as if he were communicating to a flighty child. "I think you should reconsider your decision."

Abstractedly, Jacinda brushed her fingers through her froth of hair. Perhaps his problem was that he wasn't used to dealing with female professionals. Once she explained her credentials, he would surely realize she knew her business. "Mr. Fortner—Eric— I have both a bachelor's and a master's degree in electrical engineering. From M.I.T.," she added, but

15

he gave no sign of recognition. Did he even know where or what that was? He certainly didn't seem to; he simply sat listening politely and now and then jiggling the knot of his tie as if it were choking him. She pursued doggedly. "I've worked in this field for five years, and I'm generally considered to be good at what I do." With a softening smile, she added, "I know there is a slight chance that I'm wrong." She thought it was very slight. "But I think I'm qualified to make intelligent judgments."

He shrugged dispassionately. "Everyone makes mistakes."

Honestly, he was exasperating! Jacinda looked down at her folded hands and bit her lip. She was as reasonable as the next person and she would have liked to help him, but she couldn't take the risk of damaging her company's expensive equipment.

He leaned forward. His eyes were liquid brown and serious now, compelling her to meet his gaze. "Look, I'm not trying to give you a hard time."

She arched her eyebrows questioningly; she had been beginning to wonder about that. "No?"

"No." His smile was easy, almost intimate. He ran his hands through his hair, back to where it touched the collar of his shirt and curled slightly. He really was handsome. "I'm just saying that you may have misread my plans. Maybe you've never seen anything like them before."

Jacinda could feel her face flushing, but she pushed back her anger. "Mr. Fortner—"

16

A lock of blond hair spilled over onto his forehead and he pushed it away with a large, tanned hand. "Since it's too technical for you to understand from the plans, why don't you come out to my house and let me show you a model?"

She gasped, then abandoned cool professionalism and pounded on the desk. "Too technical! Who do you think you're talking to? I don't need to see a model. I can read blueprints just fine, thank you!"

He smiled blandly, unfazed by her anger. "Hey," he said gently, "there's no reason to go rapping on the woodwork like a ghost at a seance. I'll take your word that you're competent."

"Competent! And how did *you* get to be such an expert in the field?"

"I've read a lot," he said simply.

"I mean what college did you attend?" she demanded. If Eric Fortner expected to convince her he knew what he was doing, he'd better have a degree from a first-rate university.

"I didn't," he said simply. "In fact, I didn't finish high school."

Jacinda stared at him blankly, then sank back in her chair, momentarily at a loss for words. "But . . . then how do you know anything about electrical engineering?"

He lifted his shoulders indifferently. "Oh, I picked up a little here and a little there."

"A little here . . ." Her words trailed away. In the week she had been in Arkansas, she had come to realize that people here took life at a slower pace and viewed things differently than she. But no reasonable person, in whatever part of the country, could hope to learn engineering in such a haphazard way.

"Since we're not getting anywhere here, why don't we go out to my house and look at the model?" Eric put his hands on the arms of the chair and pushed himself out of it. Standing over her desk, he looked even taller than before. As he bent forward and put his hands on her desk, she could see the bulge of muscle through his shirt.

"My truck is just outside," he continued. "I can run you out to my house and have you back in a couple of hours."

She shook her head, still slightly dazed.

"Tomorrow, then," he suggested.

"I'm sorry." She was still shaking her head slowly, almost mechanically. Seeing the model couldn't possibly make any difference. She would explain that to Lann and write Eric a very nice letter telling him why she had to reject his proposal. Jacinda rose to signal that the meeting was over and moved toward the door.

"All right." He smiled at her on the way out. His eyes rested on her face a moment, then dropped lower and his smile deepened, as if he approved of what he saw. "Thank you for your time. I look forward to hearing from you."

"It was nice meeting you, Eric."

After the door had closed behind him, Jacinda

leaned against it. Eric Fortner had no qualifications for designing anything more complex than a toothpick. He didn't even have a high school diploma! She should be glad that he was gone. Yet, absurdly, the room seemed empty without him. He had exuded a certain rustic charm that intrigued her. And he had an undefinable male mystique—a combination of the big hands, the long legs, the deep tan, and the winning smile—that quickened her interest. Although he obviously had some rough edges, he wasn't crude or gruff. She'd liked that about him. And the fact that—

She blinked as someone pushed against the door from the other side.

"Jacinda?"

"Oh, come in." Suddenly self-conscious, she smoothed her hands over her silk blouse and moved away from the door.

Lann entered. "What did you and Eric decide?" he asked cheerfully.

She circled back to her desk. Lann obviously hoped something satisfactory had been worked out. He was such a nice person, she hated to disappoint him. It occurred to her he knew something about Eric that he wasn't telling her. It would be just like Lann to try to help because Eric needed the money.

"Well?" he pressed.

Jacinda sank into her chair with a sigh. There was no point in evasion. "Look, Lann, I know you'd like to see this plan put into operation, but I'm afraid Eric Fortner doesn't know what he's doing."

He gestured toward the papers on her desk. "He sent in some fairly detailed information, didn't he?"

She dismissed that with a wave of her hand. "He could have copied it from some technical journal, maybe even *Popular Science*. Anyway, he told me himself he's had no formal training. He's built a model or something and apparently has convinced himself it will work," she ended vaguely.

Lann paused in the act of raking his fingers through his hair. "A model," he repeated. "That sounds good. Why don't you take a look at it and tell him what the problem is?" He rubbed his large palms together and smiled, happy in the knowledge that everything had been resolved.

"Well, I—"

"Eric is a local inventor of some renown," he continued. "He was written up in the paper a few months ago."

"Hmmm," she answered. Obviously there was no way out of further contact with Eric Fortner. She doubted she could make the plan work, even before she saw the model. But she wasn't exactly dreading going to look at it.

Eric chuckled softly to himself as he followed the gravel road toward his house outside of Fayetteville. So Jacinda North didn't think his plan would work. His chuckle deepened. That was the least of it. By the time he'd left, he was pretty sure she'd chalked him up as a loose screw. Telling her he hadn't finished high school hadn't advanced his cause any. His grin became more reflective as he followed the winding road downward into a ravine.

No, he hadn't graduated. School had been difficult for him from the very beginning. He never had acquired the knack of adjusting his pace to that of the other students. Once his curiosity was caught, he simply went ahead on his own. Chemistry and physics had been his favorites, and they still intrigued him.

Although he had quit school before taking those courses, he had conducted his own experiments in his parents' garage. His mother had been a little doubtful about that—especially after a minor explosion—but his father had exuded confidence. A second-generation German who still talked with a crusty accent, Eric's father had his own ideas about education and he heartily believed in the self-made man.

As Eric guided his pickup over a wooden bridge and started up a steep hill, his thoughts returned to the woman at the power company. Jacinda North had been surprisingly pretty with those luminous gray eyes, delicate features, and milk-and-honey complexion.

But she presented a problem to him. He would have to convince her she was wrong before he could get his plan approved. On that point, at least, he was determined. He had every intention of pursuing this matter until he did get approval. Admittedly, electricity was a new area of interest for him. He hadn't really begun reading up on it until a few months ago. But it had captured his imagination and he intended to see his plan implemented. He was convinced that could be accomplished by conveying to Jacinda a few things she hadn't yet learned about her field. Tactfully, of course.

A tiny field mouse scurried across the road in front of him and he braked for it. When she came out to look at his model, he'd be more careful about her feelings. She'd been rankled by his suggestion that she wasn't qualified to judge his plans. He knew he shouldn't have antagonized her. Yet, somehow, it had been impossible to stop himself. She had seemed so starched and professional sitting behind that big desk that he'd felt compelled to see her more human side. And he was glad he had succeeded in bringing it to the surface. He'd liked the flash of spirit beneath that layer of reserve.

Eric chuckled aloud again as he reflected that she must have labeled him an uneducated hick. Well, he was about to show her how charming and persuasive an Arkansas bumpkin could be when he set out to get something he wanted.

CHAPTER TWO

Although it was rush hour, to Jacinda the traffic looked mild. As she sat in her rented blue car, waiting at a stop light, she glanced around. Fayetteville, with its 35,000 souls, was the largest city in the area. It sat nearly at the center of the Ozarks, which, by precise definition weren't tall enough to be considered mountains. But the timbered ridges that rolled to the horizon loomed high and the rivers and creeks sculpted through the hills were etched deeply.

She brought her gaze from the hills back to the downtown section of Fayetteville. Centered around the square were old brick buildings shuffling up next to airy new glass and concrete structures. An old building of mellow brick sat in the middle of the square. Jacinda suspected it had once been the courthouse but now was a trendy restaurant. From where she sat waiting she could see the University of Arkansas campus sitting on a roll of hills to the northwest of downtown. Philip was going to show her around the campus sometime this week.

She gazed again at the gorgeous scenery. Smiling, she wondered if Jim Peters still thought it had been his pastoral ramblings about the beauty of the Arkansas hills that had convinced her to accept the temporary position. It hadn't been, of course. What had decided her was the promise of a promotion upon her return to New York. But now that she was here, she wasn't sure even a raise was worth spending six months in Arkansas.

When Philip had taken her for a drive through the area surrounding the town, she had been impressed at first by the walls of limestone bluffs, the deep forest gorges swathed in ferns, and the occasional slender waterfall. She had thought it pristine and primeval. But the sparsely populated hills had also been vaguely unsettling. She wasn't used to such isolation. Without the chatter of people and hum of machines she soon began to feel an overpowering sense of aloneness.

When she had mentioned that to Philip, he had smiled. "I know what you mean. I felt it myself at first. But you get used to the fact there aren't eleven million people between you and the great outdoors."

But she wondered if she ever could.

The traffic around her began to move and Jacinda followed the curving street toward the apartment she had subleased at the edge of town. As she guided the car down a sloping hill, her thoughts returned to Eric Fortner and she felt a pang of sympathy for him. Even though his plan wasn't feasible, it was plain he had put a lot of work into it. And he probably did need the money the power company would pay for the surplus electricity. Was money at the heart of the reason Lann was sending her out to Eric's?

Whatever the situation, she reflected with an audible sigh, next week she was going to look at his model. In her mind Jacinda already pictured his house as a rustic cabin complete with a calico cat sleeping beside an outdoor pump and a weathered lean-to next to the house. Country. That's what Eric was through and through. Still, he did have a nice smile and there was mischief in those cocoa eyes that could make even a city girl catch her breath.

After parking her car in the lot of her tiny apartment complex, she walked to the last of the eight units. Once inside, she tossed her purse onto a chair and glanced around. The apartment had come furnished with a brown and beige Herculon sofa, tan waffle-knit drapes, and shapeless tables that gave the room an impersonal feel. Her own apartment in New York was done in warm peach and oranges and she felt a rush of longing for it.

Through the open drapes she could see house roofs tucked in among the undulating hills. Beyond them lay wilderness. Here and there a tree was already touched with flame, an early September reminder that fall was on its way.

Fall. And then winter and spring before she could go home. She should never have come, she chided herself again. She was too "city" to adapt to this rural setting. At least she hadn't left anyone behind in New York. She and Seth had stopped dating over a month before. Seth had been a brittle wit and wickedly funny, but in the end he had proven far more interested in his law practice than in her. Not that she hadn't been aware of that for some time. So why had she let things between them drag out for so long?

Probably because of Tony. She sank onto the sofa and cupped her chin in her hands. It had been almost a relief not to be deeply involved after Tony. But she was stronger now and ready for a relationship. Perhaps Philip was the right man for that relationship. He was certainly attractive enough, and he dressed well in cashmere sweaters and hand-tailored wool suits. She closed her eyes and thought about Philip's leavetaking last night. He had stood at the door, looking down at her for a long moment. Then their mouths had met in a tentative, exploratory kiss. Although his lips had moved over hers with the right warmth and the right pressure, nothing had happened.

Jacinda swept her hand impatiently across her brow and opened her eyes. Well, what did she expect to happen? The world wasn't going to spin backward on its axis when the perfect man kissed her. But given a little time, she thought she and Philip could become very compatible. Once that happened, his kisses would surely ignite more fire.

* * *

26

The next few days went by quickly. Too quickly. Jacinda dreaded to see Friday come. Philip was going out of town for the weekend to give a guest lecture at a seminar in Omaha. That left her facing the prospect of two whole days of trying to amuse herself in Fayetteville.

Friday afternoon she was clearing her desk when Lann stopped at her door. "Busy tonight?"

"Not really. Why?"

"I was hoping you could do me a favor. The wife and I are in charge of our school's PTA carnival to raise funds for new gym equipment. We're a little shorthanded and could use help at the booths."

A school carnival? Well, it wouldn't be the World's Fair but it would be something to do.

"It starts at seven tonight. Be a great opportunity for you to meet some folks, and we really could use some extra hands," he cajoled her.

Jacinda smiled. "I'd be glad to."

"Good. Masie and I will pick you up at six. See you then." The rotund little man disappeared and she finished straightening her desk.

She was halfway home before she realized she was humming to herself. Two weeks in Arkansas and already the thought of a school carnival filled her with pleasure. She began to laugh. Glancing up, she saw a man in a car beside her watching her. He waved and she waved gaily back. "I may go country on you after all, Jim," she warned her absent boss.

The man beside her rolled his window down. "What?"

"Nothing. I was talking to myself."

"Oh." He gazed at her appreciatively, obviously wanting to continue the conversation. "Are you from Europe?"

"No."

"Oh. You have a funny accent. I thought it might be foreign."

"New York," she said briskly. The light changed and she sped away. Foreign, indeed! But even that began to strike her as funny, and she was chuckling to herself by the time she reached her apartment.

After slipping out of her tailored office clothes, she put on a flowing green silk skirt and a matching blouse that draped loosely around her neck and shoulders. She suspected it wasn't the right thing to wear to a school carnival, but she was just as sure she had nothing that was. She had been surprised to discover that her red and white striped sweater with generous raglan sleeves and short red skirt had drawn stares when she had debarked in Fayetteville. The outfit hadn't merited even a glance at La-Guardia. In New York she had bought her clothes for style and comfort and they had always blended with the crowd there. Here they were yet another sign that she was out of place.

In the bathroom she added a touch of blusher to her high cheekbones and rolled pale pink lipstick over her lips. Then she stared at her reflection. Gray eyes looked back from beneath full brows and her thick mane of hair framed her face. She had just added a pair of gold hoop earrings when the doorbell sounded.

"Coming." She trailed through the living room, slipping on her sandals as she went. At the door, she looked through the peephole with New York caution before opening it. "Hi, Lann."

"Hey, Jacinda. Ready?"

"Yes." She picked up her soft leather purse and followed him to a burgundy station wagon.

A short, plump woman with tightly curled hair and a wide smile sat in the middle of the front seat. "Hi, I'm Masie. Lann's told me all about you. I'm so glad you could come tonight. I hope he didn't force you into it." She patted her husband's knee fondly as he drove out onto the street.

Jacinda grinned. "He didn't. I'm glad to help. But I'll be honest, I've never been to anything like this before, and I don't know quite what to expect."

"Oh, you'll have fun." Masie now patted Jacinda's knee. "We've got booths for selling homemade jam, potholders, things like that. And lots of games. You know, hit the bull's-eye and dunk the teacher, that kind of thing. And grab bags for the little kids. You'll love it."

Jacinda nodded agreeably. "I'm sure I will." And it was a chance to get out of her apartment.

"I'll introduce you around to some of the other

women," Masie said. "I don't suppose you've met many people since you moved to town, have you?"

"Not many." In fact, outside of work, she had met exactly one—Philip. In New York she had lots of friends and she missed their companionship. But they had been professional women and had had much in common with her. She wasn't sure she'd know what to talk about with an Arkansas mother.

"Here we are." Lann parked beside a large, flat-roofed building and Jacinda helped carry in sacks from the back of the station wagon.

"Prizes," Masie explained as they stepped into the gym. She waved to several other women and then began emptying the sacks and setting small packages on a table. "Go ahead and look around, dear."

Jacinda did, moseying past stands selling raffle tickets for exquisitely stitched homemade quilts, a ring toss, a game for throwing darts at balloons, a woodcarver's stand, and two dozen other games and booths. At one end of the gym Lann was laboring with several other men to haul a small booth into the room.

"Do you have anyone to work in that?" Masie's voice echoed hollowly down the nearly empty gym.

"Not yet."

"Ellen had volunteered to, but she's come down with a cold," a woman at a nearby table reported.

"I'll do it," Jacinda said. It was a small booth, large enough for only one person to stand in. Obviously it was the stand for selling tickets.

Masie turned a brilliant smile on her. "Oh, dear, how sweet of you. You're so pretty; you'd be perfect." In a louder voice she called to Lann. "We have a volunteer who's going to make us a fortune." To the women in the nearby booth, she added, "Watch out for your husbands, girls."

Jacinda looked at her quizzically. "Why do you say—"

"Move aside, Jacinda." Lann and the other two men moved by, huffing and cursing softly. She looked at the writing over the top, peering closer to discern the words written in scrolls and flourishes. Then she froze.

"Kissing booth!" She shook her head. "I'm sorry. I thought . . . Well, I definitely don't want to be in a kissing booth."

The two men glanced at each other, then at Jacinda while women at the nearby booths looked over curiously.

Finally Masie said bravely, "I'll do it." She touched her curly hair with exaggerated gentility. "No doubt the men will beat each other with clubs to get to me." She smiled at Jacinda. "Do you mind watching my booth?"

"I'd love to," Jacinda said quickly and escaped behind it just as the doors opened and people began to trickle in. For the next hour she was busy selling homemade breads and cakes and home-canned foods to the people who crowded around her stand. The gym had filled with people and the noise level had

31

swelled to a steady roar. Her customers became a blur of faces as Jacinda worked as swiftly as possible, apologizing when she shortchanged one customer and accepting the money back graciously when she gave too much change to another. But no one was rude and she was actually enjoying her job. And watching Masie.

At the booth nearby, the short, plain woman leaned forward and solicited shamelessly. "Come here, Fred. Laura'll turn her head. Won't you, dear? Only a dollar, Fred."

Fred laid down his dollar, kissed Masie chastely on the cheek, and disappeared with a laughing Laura.

"Bill," Masie trilled to an old man who looked up and gave a toothless grin. "Yes, you!" He shook his head and walked away, still grinning.

"You're losing your touch, Masie," a woman at the next stand teased.

"That's because they can't see my great legs behind this booth."

Jacinda turned her attention back to her own work, accepting a twenty-dollar bill from one man and a five-dollar bill from another. She gave them their purchases and made change quickly.

"I didn't intend to tip quite that generously." Jacinda looked up into clear brown eyes. Eric Fortner was standing on the other side of the counter holding a jar of homemade pickles. In his outstretched palm he held four one-dollar bills. "I gave you a twenty."

"Oh, I'm sorry!"

"You gave me his change." A young girl exchanged her fistful of money for Eric's four dollars and disappeared into the crowd. Eric remained.

"You look like you could use some help," he said.

"She can." Masie appeared beside Jacinda and began transacting business with high-handed good humor. "Hold your horses, Ivan. I've only got two hands, terrific looking though they might be." To Eric she said, "Why don't you take the poor girl on a tour of the exhibits? She hasn't been out of this booth all evening."

"All right," he agreed amiably.

Jacinda looked into his brown eyes and nodded mutely. She had forgotten how strong his presence was. Now she found herself gazing at him to the exclusion of everyone else in the gymnasium. His blond hair was wind-ruffled and he was wearing a pair of faded blue jeans and a blue cambric shirt. He looked much more at ease in these clothes than he had in the ones he had worn to her office. She felt strangely excited standing beside him. Was it because of the carnival atmosphere, the gleeful shouts of the children, or the pressure of his hand as he took hers? She didn't try to answer that question as she joined him on the other side of the booth.

His eyes skimmed over her appraisingly as they

started through the crowd. "You're looking very pretty tonight."

"Thank you." She glanced down at her swirling silk skirt and loose blouse and then at the knee-length cotton skirts and demure blouses the women around her wore. She saw women occasionally glancing at her, but Eric didn't seem to notice. Or perhaps, it suddenly struck her, the women were looking at *him.* After all, Eric was one of them, and to the women of Fayetteville he undoubtedly looked very good. As a matter of fact, he looked quite attractive to her right now too. His hair gleamed like flax under the strong lights and his smile had the power to make any woman seem very special.

He nodded to people they passed and put his hand lightly around her waist. "So, tell me about New York. Do emigrants still come to Ellis Island?"

She stared up at him. "No, it's been closed since—" Was he teasing her? She could have sworn she saw a twinkle in his eye. On the other hand, this was such a remote area and Eric probably wasn't very well read. He might still harbor misconceptions about New York.

"What about the alligators in the sewer system?" he asked lazily. "Pretty thick, huh?"

He was definitely fighting back a grin. The sneak! "My goodness, yes," she said soberly. "Big game hunters go on safaris into the sewers all the time. Now, tell me about Arkansas, is it true that most of the people here have one leg shorter than the other from walking up the hills?"

"It's true." A slow smile dawned. "I'd be glad to show you my legs later if you'd like to see for yourself."

For an instant a very provocative picture flashed through her mind. She might have pondered it longer, but she saw that he was watching for her reaction. With a shake of her head, she laughed softly. "You, sir, are what my grandmother used to call a rascal." But a very appealing one at that. What had she thought was wrong with him when he had come to her office? she mused. At this moment everything about him seemed very right. His arm around her waist had just the right pressure, and when he bent to speak to her his shoulder grazed hers companionably. Small things, but still . . .

Eric pulled her to a stop beside a booth. "Would you like to buy a raffle ticket for a quilt?"

"Nice for your hope chest, dear," the elderly woman selling tickets joined in.

Jacinda fingered a quilt with a large star forming the central pattern while Eric bought a ticket.

"Well, hello there." A pretty brunette tapped Eric on the shoulder.

"Hi, Stacey."

When he grinned at the other woman, Jacinda felt a stab of disappointment. She knew it was absurd and childish, but she didn't like not having his full attention.

The slender woman smiled. "Haven't seen you lately."

"I've been busy at the quarry." Eric turned to Jacinda. "This is Stacey Jones. She's a secretary at the high school. Stacey, this is Jacinda. She's an engineer with the power company."

The two women exchanged polite comments.

"I don't hear any Arkansas twang in your voice," Stacey laughed. "Did you just move here?"

"Yes. I'm only going to be in Fayetteville for six months, then I go back to New York."

"Well, I hope you like it." Stacey's smile was friendly, but when she turned to Eric it became softer. "Don't be such a stranger. Come by and visit sometime. You know you're always welcome."

He nodded agreeably and Jacinda wondered if he would visit Stacey. There must be a lot of places in Fayetteville where he was welcome, she considered, and the thought disturbed her.

"How about something to eat?" Eric asked.

"Sounds good." Jacinda put thoughts of Stacey from her mind as he took her arm and they started through the crowd.

He bought a caramel-covered apple on a stick and they took turns eating it. When he reached over to wipe a dab of caramel from her lip, she playfully bit at his finger. At that moment the action around them seemed to stop, and she was looking up into a pair of thoughtful brown eyes and studying an expression that was half puzzlement, half pleasure. He drew his finger slowly away from her mouth, rolling it almost seductively over the gentle curve of her bottom lip. The moment ended and she drew away. What was she doing flirting with Eric like this? To begin with, her association with him was a business one. Secondly, they had totally different backgrounds and very little in common. And the sooner she put some distance between them, the better.

With a busy gesture she brushed back her hair. "I must get back to help Masie. You go ahead and look around. Thanks for the candy apple." She flitted a wave at him and retreated. She couldn't deny that she found Eric very attractive tonight, but surely that was because she was far from home and lonely. She knew nothing could ever develop between them. After all, she liked men who were interested in good books and classical music and furthering their careers.

Jacinda was well beyond Masie's booth before she realized she had passed it. Pivoting, she started back. Lann was standing in the kissing booth, looking sheepish but game. "Come on, Karen. Give me a bit of a kiss. I'll never tell Frank. You know I won't."

A saucy Karen shook her head. "I'm saving my money in case Robert Redford shows up."

Jacinda stopped and leaned against the booth. "How's business?"

"Lousy. Even Masie was doing better than I am."

"I heard that!" his wife yelled.

"Why don't you try your hand at it?" Lann suggested to Jacinda.

She smiled. "I wouldn't object to trying my hand. It's my cheeks and lips I don't want to donate. I'd feel funny letting strangers kiss me."

He waved his hand around the room dismissively. "These aren't strangers. I've known them all my life. Do you think I'd be offering up my virtue lightly?" Lann was out of the booth now and gently pushing her toward the door. "Come on. It's all in the name of charity."

Jacinda laughed, sighed, and then nodded in agreement. "Tomorrow I'm definitely checking myself in for observation."

"That's fine," he said easily. "We'll get you some sort of compensation from the power company. Good girl. I'll just look in on Masie and be right back."

Jacinda didn't solicit and she had no customers for the first five minutes, although a man or two did throw her an interested glance. Finally, a nice-looking middle-aged man stepped up. He paid the dollar and kissed her on the cheek, which encouraged others to try.

One or two brushed her lips lightly, but most were timidly correct in their kisses in spite of such unrefined exhortations from their fellows as "Sock it to her, Don!" or "Lay a big one on 'er!" She had grown quite calm in her wanton position until Eric stopped in front of the booth.

He rested an elbow on the counter in front of her. "Do you make house calls?"

Excitement fluttered within, but she matched his casualness. "Afraid not."

"Oh." She watched him push his fingers through his hair, leaving a wake of tiny furrows in it. Then he took out his wallet.

At that moment her breathing wasn't quite regular. It hadn't made her nervous for strangers to kiss her, but the thought of Eric kissing her did. Would he merely touch her cheek or would he kiss her full on the lips? She ran her tongue over her dry lips and waited in anticipation.

Eric fingered the money in his hand, looking down at it as if he had forgotten what he had intended to do with it.

Suddenly her nervousness was washed away and replaced with a dismaying thought. He wasn't going to kiss her. And she wanted him to very much. Jacinda couldn't have explained, even to herself, her tangled reasoning. All she knew was that he looked tall and appealing and disturbingly masculine. And she had some half formed notions of a need to be in his arms.

Finally he looked up. His gaze on hers was steadily intent as he asked quietly, "Do you mind if I kiss you?"

"No, I—I'd like that," she breathed.

She tilted her head up as he bent to graze her lips with his. Then her long lashes fluttered downward.

At first their lips touched softly, then melted together. She tasted caramel and something less easily identified—a leashed desire that could have been his or might have been her own. He drew closer and his mouth became more insistent on hers. A feeling of yearning began to spread within her like the rays of the sun. Then the reassuring pressure of his mouth and the sweet taste was gone. He drew back and stretched out a hand to tuck back a disheveled curl.

Someone else pressed a cold kiss on her cheek after that, but Jacinda barely noticed. She was enveloped in a fuzzy blanket of contentment. Long after Eric had pressed her hand and moved away, she tried to follow him through the crowd. Finally the blond head was lost and she concluded with a sinking feeling that he had left. The gym gradually cleared.

"Dear." Someone touched her arm.

Jacinda blinked and then looked up at Masie.

"Are you ready to go?"

"Yes." She followed obediently, her body moving of its own accord while her mind remained elsewhere.

"I thought we had a good crowd. I think we made a lot of money," Masie said.

"Ummm." Had it meant anything to Eric? Or had it been a simple kiss to him, and she a light flirtation for the evening?

Masie chatted nonstop as she ushered Jacinda out to the car. "Did you see Christopher, Lann? My, but

40

he's getting fat. Of course, all the Warners run to fat. Come along, dear."

"What runs in Eric Fortner's family?" Jacinda asked curiously.

"Money."

CHAPTER THREE

Monday night Philip sat beside Jacinda on the sofa swirling the ice cubes in his drink. His brown hair was perfectly in place and his blue polo shirt matched his eyes. "Omaha was a dead bore. The speakers talked on and on while half the students fell asleep in their chairs. Couldn't blame them." He turned to her. "How was your weekend?"

"Fine." She smiled reflectively. "Friday night I helped sell jam and potholders at a school carnival." Although she wasn't exactly embarrassed about the kissing booth, for some reason she didn't mention it.

He chuckled. "Seriously, Jacinda, what did you do?"

She stared, mildly affronted. "Seriously, I went to a school carnival."

Philip gazed at her for a moment in silence. "Well, when in Rome . . . Although I'd hardly call this Rome," he added dryly. "How was it?"

"It was fun. In fact, I had a great time." Some events of that evening stood out much more clearly than others. She curled and uncurled her bare toes on the soft carpeting as she thought of candied apples, quiet smiles, and one unsettling kiss.

"I suppose it might be interesting to go once. The problem with these folksy diversions is that they become old very quickly."

"You're probably right," she agreed mildly.

He glanced at his watch. "Gad, is it that late? I've got to run; I have an early class in the morning. Maybe we can get together tomorrow night for dinner?" he said hopefully.

Jacinda shook her head. "I don't think tomorrow will be a good day for me." First thing in the morning she was going to Eric's to look at the model. And she dreaded it. Friday night she had put business aside and had enjoyed herself with him. But tomorrow she would be the professional woman again, and she was going to have to tell Eric the hard truth.

At her office he had not accepted her rejection of his plan. This time it would be final and she would make very sure he understood that. But it was going to be harder now that she knew him better. At least she wouldn't have to feel guilty because she thought he needed the money, she consoled herself. Masie had told her Eric was the only son of a farmer who had shrewdly invested in Oklahoma land and now owned several oil wells.

Philip finished his wine and rose. "I'll call you Saturday."

She nodded and walked to the door with him.

"Good night." He drew her into his arms and grazed her lips.

She sensed he was only waiting for a sign of encouragement to deepen and intensify the kiss and though she did like Philip a lot, she didn't want to rush it. Gently, she pulled back. "Philip, I—"

"Shhh." He put his finger to her lips and smiled ruefully. "It's all right. We still don't know each other that well. I'm willing to wait." He kissed her cheek and disappeared.

Slowly she walked into the bedroom. She had hung posters of European cities on the bare walls and had bought a spread of bright blue and red flowers for the motel-type bed. After kicking off her shoes, she shed her clothes and slipped beneath the covers. Within the dark apartment, all was quiet.

From her sixth floor walkup in New York, she had been able to hear the cars on the street below, smell the gas fumes, and occasionally hear the cabbies shouting at each other. Here, the silence could be unnerving. At times it became so still, Jacinda had the scary feeling she was alone in the universe. More than once she had gotten up at night to look out the window to assure herself there was other life—a house with lights on, a car on a distant street, anything that would make her feel in touch with civilization.

Someone in another apartment turned on a stereo and she fell asleep listening to its faint, comforting sounds. But the eerie silence awoke her at two o'clock. Restlessly, Jacinda turned over in bed. She hadn't had so much trouble sleeping since her break-up with Tony four years ago. Then she had lain awake many nights agonizing over her decision. In the end she knew she had made the right choice. But that hadn't make it any less painful.

Jacinda had first been introduced to Tony by a mutual friend. They'd clicked from the beginning. Aside from being a hard-driving stockbroker, he was also a gregarious, darkly attractive Italian given to telling tall tales and cursing in his native tongue. It hadn't been long before she was in love with him and they had begun making plans to marry. The wedding arrangements had been easy to make since his aunt who ran a bakery could supply the cake and his cousin the florist could provide the flowers. She had teased Tony that he had a relative for every occasion.

Looking back, Jacinda couldn't pinpoint when she had begun to feel she was being swallowed up by Tony's family of five brothers and four sisters, dozens of aunts and uncles, and innumerable relatives. All she knew was once they became engaged, she and Tony seemed to be spending so much of their time with his family that they rarely had a day to themselves. And every member of Tony's clan apparently had more say in the wedding plans than Jacinda did.

Slowly she realized that she was facing more than a simple case of meddling in-laws. Tony never did anything without first taking a family poll. Being by nature an independent and private person, Jacinda began to resent Tony's relatives for their constant interference—and Tony for inviting his parents, cousins, aunts, and uncles to make his decisions for him.

It took a major argument over Tony asking his parents to help him choose a honeymoon spot to make Jacinda postpone the wedding. She and Tony had had long talks. He agreed with her that marriage was two people sharing their lives. He wanted to share his life with her. But he wanted to share their lives with his family as well. Finally, painfully, Jacinda admitted that Tony's sense of obligation and dependence on his family wasn't something that was going to change.

She had looked hard at the white satin gown hanging in her closet, then she had stared at herself in the mirror watching the tears course down her cheeks. She loved Tony. But already she resented his family. How was she going to feel in five years? Ten? Twenty? When was her resentment going to grow to include him and the wedge between them going to become a chasm? It seemed inevitable that someday it would.

It had ended at an impasse. Neither had been right, neither wrong—just different. But their parting had left her with a profound understanding of the importance of finding a man with whom she was compatible—a man with the same outlook on life and life-style as her own. Otherwise, she would only be courting heartache again.

* * *

At eight thirty the next morning Jacinda picked up the ivory linen jacket that matched her pleated skirt and started out the door. Yesterday Lann had given her directions to Eric's house and she now carried his hastily scrawled map in her hand. "Can't miss it," he had told her a half a dozen times. The tangled lines on the map seemed to argue otherwise and she felt like a laboratory rat being sent into a maze.

Once outside town, she turned near George's feed elevator and continued down a gravel road that soon became a rollercoaster of hills and an obstacle course of chuckholes. When she swerved to avoid one, she invariably hit another. More than once her head banged the unpadded roof of the car.

Jacinda gripped the wheel tighter as the car jolted along. While gathering up papers at her office this morning, she had again become aware of a fact that had slipped to the back of her mind Friday night: Eric wasn't even a high school graduate and he had no credentials in electrical engineering. She wished Lann hadn't asked her to come out here today. After seeing a different, very compelling side of Eric at the carnival, she didn't want to play the heavy and shatter his dream. But she had to do her job.

As she swerved to avoid a particularly deep hole, it dawned on her she hadn't seen a house for some time. Uncomfortably, she looked around. She didn't like being out in the country alone. Worse, she seemed to have been driving a long time. Had she missed a turn? Was she lost? Around her she saw nothing but fields and woods and hills for miles. The feeling of isolation grew stronger.

It was ten nerve-racking minutes later before she rounded a curve and saw a mailbox with E.F. lettered on it. Relieved, she whipped into the driveway, then paused and stared at the house. Half of the natural stone house was earth-sheltered and tastefully butted into a hillside. Well-placed shrubs landscaped the yard. This was far more contemporary than she would have associated with Eric.

Jacinda slid out and walked to the front door. It was opened before she even knocked.

Eric smiled at her. "Ah, it's the lady with the funny accent."

"Sorry I'm late." She smoothed her hair to keep from looking into his chocolate brown eyes. Now that she was here, she wished even more fervently she didn't have to let him down. He must be desperately hopeful his plan would be approved. Lann had told her Eric had devoted a lot of time to formulating it.

"No problem," he assured her. "Come on in."

She followed him inside, stopping in the living room to look around. It was a large room with natural wood floors, forest green canvas chairs and sectional sofa, white throw rugs, and smoked glass tables. Ferns hung from the beams and a stained glass window in the ceiling prismed in light. It was beautiful, and light years from the country look she had expected. "I—your house is lovely."

"Thanks." He seemed pleased by her approval. "Why don't you come downstairs and see my work area?"

She followed him to the back of the living room where a spiral staircase wound down to an immense room with one wall given over completely to windows. Half of the room served as a recreation area, with a cozy corner for watching television, an antique pool table topped with a slate bed, and a bar. The rest of the room was an orderly work area with simple laboratory equipment. She looked around curiously.

"Is anything wrong?" he asked. "You seem a little surprised."

"I am surprised." She glanced up at him, smiling self-consciously. "Your house isn't what I'd expected." Eric Fortner seemed to be a man full of surprises. Judging from that crooked half smile, he knew it and was enjoying himself.

"It wasn't what I'd expected either," he said easily. "I asked for a three-bedroom ranch house, but when I came back, this was what the contractor had built."

"I see." His teasing grin made her momentarily forget business. He was dressed in khaki trousers and a blue cotton shirt casually open at the neck. The sleeves were rolled up to reveal a sinewy, tanned arm. He was attractive. If she were an Arkansas woman, she could have been very interested. But she wasn't an Arkansas woman, she reminded herself. She was a New Yorker, a visitor in this state, and she was about to be the bearer of bad news. Jacinda was just getting ready to ask to see the model when the doorbell rang.

He glanced upward. "That must be my neighbor. He's interested in buying my pickup. Come on up and I'll introduce you."

She trailed after him back up the winding stairs. Eric opened the front door.

"Hi, Buford." He turned toward Jacinda. "Buford, I'd like you to meet Jacinda North. She works for the power company."

She smiled at the middle-aged man who had a toothpick inserted in one corner of his mouth. He grinned back at her. "Nice to meet you, ma'am. Should I come back later to see the truck, Eric?"

"Well, maybe—"

Jacinda interrupted. "I don't mind waiting." In fact, she felt she had been given a reprieve from having to face the moment when she gave Eric the verdict.

He shrugged. "Okay. This way, Buford. You might as well come too," he said over his shoulder to Jacinda.

They walked to the attached garage and Eric lifted the door. Jacinda stepped inside. A blue and white truck, its chrome polished to a gleam, sat in the center of the neat garage.

Buford walked around the truck critically. "How old you say it is?"

"Four years old."

"I'll say this for you, fella, you take good care of your machines." Buford paused to push the toothpick more firmly into his mouth, then raised the hood. "Yep, you sure do."

Curious, Jacinda strolled to the front of the truck and peered into the engine beside him. For an engine, it looked very clean.

"So you're going to buy a car, huh?" Buford asked.

"Yep. I've never owned one, so I figure it's about time. 'Course I'll still have the quarry truck."

The other man nodded absently. "You give guarantees?"

Eric rested his elbows on the front fender and smiled. "Sure do. The Oklahoma City guarantee. If it breaks in two, you own both pieces."

The other man chuckled. "That's what I figured."

"If you want it, Bufe, you'd better buy it today. I've got several people who're real interested."

Did he? Jacinda wondered and knew the answer when he winked at her. It was a small gesture, but it made her feel as if they shared a special secret. Her mind floated back to his kiss at the carnival. It, too, had made her feel she was more to him than a casual acquaintance.

Buford practically disappeared beneath the hood,

muttering something about spark plugs.

"I'll put in new spark plugs if you like," Eric said.

"Good. I like a man who stands behind what he sells." Buford raised his head and chuckled. " 'Course, I guess all salesmen stand behind what they sell; some just stand farther behind than others." He straightened. "Well, I suppose I'll take it. You say you want twenty-five hundred?"

Eric laughed. "I said three thousand, but I'll take more."

As she watched them bargain, Jacinda realized how completely at ease the two men felt with each other. Theirs was the kind of camaraderie that came from having known each other a long time. Suddenly she felt very much the outsider. In New York she had sometimes seen tourists venturing cautiously into the subways, looking lost and out of place as they studied their maps. Watching them had made her feel almost smug about her own knowledge of the city. Now she was the one on unfamiliar territory, the one who didn't quite fit in, and she didn't like the feeling.

". . . I'll bring the title over tomorrow."

"Great, see you then." Buford nodded to Jacinda. "Nice meeting you, ma'am," he said before he disappeared.

Eric put the hood down and they started back toward the house. "Before we get into business, I have something for you." He led the way back into the house, opened a cedar chest, and pulled out a handmade quilt. "Here."

She hesitated, searching for a polite way of rejecting the gift. Accepting a present from Eric was the last thing she should be doing right now. The very thoughtfulness of the gesture made her uncomfortable. Suddenly she wanted to get her business over with and leave.

"Go on, take it," he urged. "I won it at the raffle."

"But it's yours." She didn't want anything that would tie her to Eric. And she particularly didn't want any reminders of the carnival.

He bundled the quilt into her arms. "I bought the ticket for you. I want you to have it."

"Well, I—thank you." She couldn't very well throw it on the floor, she considered as she looked down at it and touched a row of perfectly matched hand stitches. And it was lovely. "Someone put a lot of work into this," she murmured. He was looking at her and she knew she should show more enthusiasm, but she felt awkward. If a good friend had given her the quilt, she would have kissed them spontaneously. But that didn't seem appropriate under these circumstances. She avoided his gaze as she set the quilt on the sofa. "Well," she said briskly, "let's go see your model."

After a moment's quizzical study, he shrugged. "It's outside."

Jacinda followed him out a back door where a

balmy September breeze stirred through the oaks and hickories. He walked ahead of her and led the way down a gentle incline. Gradually it grew steeper until it was a dramatic slope. Jacinda paused uncertainly. Her shoes were both backless and strapless, not exactly made for scaling down hills. Although she didn't want to take the chance of falling, she wasn't sure she wanted Eric helping her either. The more distance she could maintain between them, the better.

He turned back to her. "Coming?"

Common sense overcame her reservations. "I hate to admit this, but I need a hand. I'm afraid I'll slip."

His eyes widened as he looked at her shoes. "In those things I wouldn't be surprised. Wait there." He climbed back up the hill and secured an arm around her waist.

She was here strictly on business and she had always been a very professional person, she reminded herself. Then why was she so conscious of the crisp lime scent of his aftershave? And when he tightened his arm around her and their hips touched, why did she feel that thrill of pleasure? As they descended, Jacinda acknowledged she was more aware of the strong arm looped around her waist than she was of the rocky slope. All too soon they reached the bottom of the hill and he released her.

"Thank you." She stared down at her shoes, more from an effort to avoid looking at him than anything else. "Even in New York these things were an impractical indulgence."

He chuckled. "I can see why. You couldn't possibly run from all those hordes of muggers in those stilts."

She shook her head with an exasperated smile. "Such misconceptions! You should come to New York sometime and see what it's *really* like."

"I may take you up on the invitation," he drawled.

She thought he was teasing, but she wasn't sure. Briskly she looked away. "I'm anxious to see your model." It was a lie, but it was a change of subject, which was what she desperately needed right now.

"Here it is." He walked several yards away and pointed proudly to a small conveyor inclined against the side of the hill. "The real one is much longer, but you can get the idea from this. At the quarry I'll use rocks to run it but the model is so small it'll work on sand."

He spoke confidently about his plans for the conveyor at the quarry. Again she realized it hadn't sunk in that he had very little chance of getting approval for his plan. His enthusiasm was touching and that made it even more difficult to think of disappointing him.

"The sand is loaded on one end and . . ." He poured sand at the top of the conveyor and it began moving down the belt, powering the generator.

This was the moment of truth. Yes, the generator

ran, she noted, but the power was certain to come in surges. Stepping over to read the amp meter on the generator, she waited for the needle to fluctuate. She'd let him down very easy, of course, carefully explaining to him the damage that could be done to the power company's equipment through current surges. The machine continued to purr like a kitten.

Five minutes later it was still running smoothly, with the needle holding steady. Jacinda was dumbfounded. Her objection to letting him tap into the power lines had been totally unfounded.

She blinked, looked at the meter again, and then shook her head in disbelief. "It really does work."

"Of course it does," Eric agreed proudly, as if there had never been the least question.

But she was so engrossed in her thoughts that she scarcely heard him. Self-reproach mingled with wounded pride. She had always been proud of the high caliber of her work. Yet this was one instance when she had been very wrong. If Lann hadn't insisted she look at the model, Eric would never have gotten his system into operation.

Jacinda groped for words. "I—I was convinced you were wrong." Swallowing, she added, "I owe you an apology."

He grinned. "For what? Because you thought I was just another backwoods tinkerer who wanted to produce electricity at a rock quarry and sell it to the power company? It was logical for you to be cautious. What matters is that you've changed your mind."

She bit her bottom lip, still chastising herself. "I was too cautious." And once she had learned he didn't have a diploma, she hadn't even been willing to look further. "I feel like an idiot. I was hasty in making my decision and close-minded once I'd made it." But how could she have been expected to recognize that Eric knew what he was talking about?

"I'll tell you what," he said casually, "I'll give you a chance to make it up to me by taking me out to dinner."

"I—" She hesitated. She liked Eric. She liked him too much, and she'd better nip this in the bud before it went it any further. Eric was as unsuited for her as Tony had been. But when she looked into his warm brown eyes, her refusal died on her lips. She owed him something after the injury she'd almost done him. And what would be the harm in a simple dinner? "All right. How about Friday night?"

"Good." His smile revealed the roguish dimple.

She smiled back. "Well, I'd better get back on the road and try to find my way back to the office. Any danger of me getting lost?"

"None. Just turn left at the brown cow." He helped her up the hill and they walked back to his house. "Don't forget your quilt."

Jacinda picked it up, then turned to look at him. Perhaps she should have thanked him for the quilt or apologized again for not giving his plan more consideration, but she merely gazed at him. His hair had been tousled by the breeze and there was a smudge on his cheek where he must have wiped it with the back of his hand while loading sand.

"Good-bye, then," he said quietly.

She hugged the quilt closer to her. "Good-bye."

CHAPTER FOUR

Eric picked up a gallon of milk and two loaves of bread on his way to the produce department. He was glad he'd resolved the matter of the conveyor. Now he could devote his full attention to running the quarry. It had been a failing operation when he had bought it three years ago, and it still wasn't as profitable as he'd like. But being able to sell electricity to the power company would help a great deal, he reflected, juggling the milk and bread while he tried to put tomatoes into a plastic bag.

"You don't want that old, shriveled tomato." A woman took it from his hand and replaced it with a plump, juicy one. "Here, this one's much better."

He grinned at her. "Thanks, Masie."

"Jacinda seems like a nice girl, doesn't she?" Masie said nonchalantly as she dropped some cucumbers into a bag.

"Yes."

"Think you'll see her again?"

"I imagine so," he drawled. "This town isn't that big."

She shot him an exasperated look. "That's not what I mean and you know it, Eric Fortner. Why don't you take the girl out? She's away from home, doesn't know many people, and I'm sure she's lonely."

He hid his smile as he hoisted the milk more securely under his arm and wrapped a twist-tie around the bag of tomatoes. Masie was addicted to matchmaking, and she'd be disappointed if he made this too easy for her. "Good price on tomatoes," he observed.

"Maybe I should mind my own business," she began in a tone that boded against that possibility, "but I thought that you and Jacinda would make a nice couple."

He chuckled. "The problem is that I'm not sure she feels the same."

Masie shot him a startled look. "Why wouldn't she? At the risk of inflating your ego, you are an attractive, personable, and—and this is the key word—*unattached* man. Any woman would be lucky to get you." She sniffed. "We both know several who've tried."

"Well," he said casually, "as it happens Jacinda is taking me out this weekend."

"*She's* taking you out?"

"Yeah. I tried to get out of it but she hounded me. Poor kid, I felt kind of sorry for her. She's probably

60

never had any excitement in her life and then she meets me and the experience has been almost too much for her."

Masie rolled her eyes. "You could fertilize our front lawn with this. Still, you're sinfully nice-looking, so I may decide to run away to South America with you myself." She plucked a potato from his hand, aghast. "You're not going to take that one. It's already sprouting!"

He shrugged. "They've usually sprouted by the time I get around to using them."

"Honestly! We must find you a woman to get your life organized. I'll work on it, but you can't expect me to do everything," she added with dignity.

"I wouldn't want you to do everything." He laughed softly. "There are certain aspects of being with a woman that I handle very nicely on my own."

She shook her finger at him. "You're an ornery, wicked man." But she didn't seem to disapprove.

Lann ambled up beside his wife and put his arm around her. "Is she trying to talk you into marrying Jacinda?"

Masie tossed her head haughtily. "Let Jacinda take care of herself. I'm making my own arrangements."

The older man exchanged teasing glances with Eric. "I'd better get her out of here. Fresh produce always brings out the scarlet woman in her."

After they had gone, Eric picked up his sack of tomatoes and started toward the cash register. Masie had always been a notorious matchmaker. Not that he had needed Masie to point out Jacinda's charms. He'd already noticed them. But he meant it when he'd said Jacinda seemed to want to keep her distance from him. He planned to do something about that, and he was going to start by changing his image a little.

After checking out, he put his groceries into his new green sedan and drove to the downtown square. The milk would have to keep while he did a little shopping. He parked outside an elegant men's shop and went in, aware that his jeans and red plaid shirt were conspicuous in the subdued environment of the store.

A stiff salesmen with a thin moustache approached him. "May I help you?"

"Yes, I'd like a suit." Eric pointed toward a headless mannequin. "Something like that." He usually wore his sports jacket on dates, but he thought Jacinda might expect more. And he wanted her to feel comfortable with him even if the damn tie did choke him.

The salesman pulled a suit off the rack and held it up with a flourish. "Here's a nice camel wool that would be excellent for this winter. It's cut in the latest style."

"I'll try it on." Eric stopped by a rack of ties. "I need a tie to go with it." He frowned at the blur of colors; he had no idea what went with camel. "Why don't you pick one out? And maybe a shirt that would look good with the suit."

"A nice white oxford would be appropriate." The salesman was warming up, relishing his role as advisor. "If I may suggest, sir, this brown argyle sweater would be splendid on less formal occasions with the suit trousers."

Eric looked at it doubtfully. "Didn't those go out in the fifties?" He didn't want to look like one of the Four Freshmen with Jacinda. He wasn't exactly an arbiter of women's fashions, but he was pretty sure her clothes were stylish.

The salesman drew himself up with dignity, affronted at having his taste called into question. "They're very trendy right now, sir. Very big on the coasts."

Eric nodded. That was good enough for him. "I'll take it."

"Wise choice. And now, if you'd care to step into the dressing room, I'll take a length on the pants."

Thursday night Philip took Jacinda to a recital at the university's school of music. Afterward, they were invited to a wine and cheese party given by one of the other faculty members. Jacinda wore gray hose and her newest dress, a pearl gray sheath. She worried that it was too dramatic, but once she arrived she began to relax. Although the female faculty members and the professors' wives were dressed more conservatively, they complimented her on her

63

outfit with genuine admiration and a hint of wistfulness. As Jacinda circulated in the antique-filled living room, she discovered that most of the people weren't natives of Arkansas.

"Well, my dear, what do you think of our little town so far?" a stocky English professor asked.

She smiled at him. "Very nice."

"I suppose so." He took time out to finish his glass of wine before continuing. "I was born in Vermont and I've never gotten used to how hot the summers are here. But I have tenure, so I stay. I understand you're here for only a few months?"

"Yes. Until spring."

"Winters aren't so great either," he mumbled. "And no one here knows how to drive in the snow."

Philip came up beside her and put his arm around her. "How about some cheese?" Once they were out of earshot, he said, "Hope you haven't been stuck with him long. He's not exactly Mr. Congeniality."

She smiled. "I don't mind. It's good just to be out with people. I've been spending a lot of time alone." As soon as the words were spoken, she regretted them. It sounded as if she were complaining that Philip had neglected her. What she really meant was that she missed her friends and family in New York.

He stopped and looked down at her, the blue eyes searching. "I could remedy that."

Jacinda smiled blandly and continued toward the refreshment table at the back of the crowded room. No doubt he could. But she didn't want to get involved too quickly. And she was going to be here long enough that they didn't have to rush into a relationship. "What do you suggest—Brie or smoked cheddar?"

"The cheddar." He leaned against the wall and watched her. "I have some good news."

She glanced up questioningly.

"I've heard from Columbia and I think I stand a good chance of getting a job there. I'll know in a couple of weeks."

"Great." She beamed at him. Columbia was in New York City, which meant they could continue to see each other when she returned home. There were no longer any obstacles in her path should she fall in love with Philip, which made everything much simpler.

Friday night, an hour before Eric was to arrive, Jacinda had half of her clothes spread out on the bed. She looked them over indecisively. The rose silk seemed too formal. The poplin skirt and madras shirt were probably right, but she wondered if she shouldn't simply wear jeans. Although she was taking Eric out to eat, she would have to depend on him to suggest the restaurant. And he might have something very casual in mind. In fact, he probably did. She doubted that he even owned any dressier clothes than the ones he had worn so awkwardly to her office. That decided her; she picked up the jeans and a red knit sweater.

"When in doubt, dress down," she murmured aloud.

Fifteen minutes later, clad in the jeans and red sweater and her hair pulled back into a ponytail, she surveyed herself in the mirror. She had added enough dark blue shadow to accent her gray eyes and was carefully applying a russet lipstick when the doorbell rang.

Quickly she brushed on blusher and hurried to the door. Once there, however, she paused to run her hands down the sweater and touch her hair. Wetting her lips, she threw the door open.

They both stared.

Eric was wearing a well-cut camel suit, white shirt, and tasteful maroon tie. His usually casual hair had been severely parted on one side, although an unruly lock was already straying toward his forehead.

He gazed in disbelief, then broke into a laugh. She laughed too. But she felt oddly moved that he had gone to so much trouble for her. The clothes even smelled new, she realized as he put an arm around her and drew her back into the apartment, still chuckling.

"It seems we have a problem," he declared.

"Yes," she murmured as he pulled her down on the sofa beside him.

Eric yanked gently on the ponytail. "This is the first thing that has to go. I like my women's hair done in a more sophisticated style," he informed her loftily.

She slipped the band off her hair and shook it. "Better?"

"Much better." His eyes moved appreciatively over the generous froth of hair. "Next the sweater will have to go." He reached down to pull it over her head. "I'm beginning to like this."

Jacinda captured his hands in hers, laughing. "Don't get to liking it too much; this is as far as you go."

Suddenly their laughter faded and they both became very still. He bent toward her at the same moment she lifted her face to his and his mouth closed over hers. It was different from the other time he had kissed her. This didn't begin with a gentle prelude that built to passion. It began with startling intensity as his tongue invaded her mouth, awakening a sense of need. She wrapped her arms around his neck and grazed the tip of his tongue with her own. She felt an electrifying sensation that fanned even more embers of desire. Their mouths clung as if each depended on the other for their life's breath.

When his mouth finally left hers it was to singe a path of kisses over to her ear. His tongue traced the shell of her ear in a way that left her breathless and yearning. She dropped her head to his neck and pressed warm kisses there while he slid his hands beneath her sweater and massaged her bare back.

The world retreated and she knew only his lips, his touch, and the scent of his aftershave.

"Jacinda?" he whispered.

She trembled at the soft feel of his breath on her ear. "Mmmm?"

"Maybe the solution to our clothes problems is for both of us to take them off. I'll go first if you'd like."

She was tempted. In the privacy of her bedroom, it wouldn't matter that he was country, she city; he a dropout, she a Phi Beta Kappa; he a member of the community, she a temporary visitor. But, of course, all those things did matter. Slowly, regretfully, she drew back. "No, I don't think that's the answer."

Her spirit was willing, but when his mouth captured hers in a languorous, intoxicating kiss, she responded instantly and eagerly. She captured his bottom lip between her teeth and bit gently. It felt good to touch that sensuously bowed lip, and when he drew her even closer and enveloped her whole mouth with his, she felt she could drown in a honeycomb of pleasure.

It wasn't supposed to be like this, she thought vaguely. She had planned tonight to be a quiet, dignified dinner, and a polite good bye. But the message her lips conveyed to him was hardly one of parting. They enticed and urged him on. She knew she should draw back, but she couldn't. It had been easy to marshal all the reasons he was unsuitable for her when she wasn't buried in the secure cave of his arms, feeling his hair dusting against her cheeks and his lips moving insistently over hers. This couldn't possibly be wrong when it felt so infinitely right. Only when she felt his hands slide beneath her sweater and his strong fingers close over the filmy material of her bra did she draw back, shaking her head to clear it of romantic notions.

"I—we'd better go eat now."

He smiled regretfully. "I was hoping you'd forget that."

Jacinda moved away from him, not trusting herself to ward off more advances. "I'll go change into something else."

"Need any help?" he asked hopefully.

"I'll manage." She escaped into her bedroom and snatched up the rose silk. She was going to have to put some distance between them this evening. When he brought her home later tonight, she wanted it understood they were nothing more than friends. How could they be more when they were so different? With a wry grimace she muttered aloud, "After an opener like that, it's going to be difficult to be polite but distant."

Ten minutes later she reappeared in the living room with her hair secured atop her head and carrying a light cream jacket. "I'm ready." She didn't meet his eyes.

He stood and ran his hands carefully over his suit. "You rumpled it something terrific," he complained.

"I'm sorry." His hair was also tousled and the temptation to smooth it was almost irresistible. But that way lay danger. She stood rigidly by the door, intent on maintaining an attitude of dignity.

Eric stopped beside the door and stared down at her quizzically. "I was kidding."

"Oh." She smiled politely.

"Anything wrong—other than my jokes?"

"Nothing's wrong. Where do you suggest we eat?"

He searched her face. "There are a couple of nice hotel restaurants. Then there's a good one in the old brick building in the middle of the square. We'll discuss it in the car." He ran his fingers through his disheveled hair. "Look, Jacinda—"

"We'd better get started, don't you think?" she said brightly. Darn, why had he dressed so specially for her? Why did he have a way of kissing her that made her forget that he was unsuitable for her? But it simply wouldn't work.

Once inside his car they drove in silence to a restaurant on the edge of town. Dark wood paneling and brass wall sconces created a mood of elegance from the moment they stepped through the door. They were shown to a table in an intimate corner of the room. The waiter lit the candle on their table and left them with their wine.

"This is very nice," she murmured. The trick, she had decided, was to look at him as little as possible. Those compelling brown eyes could make her say and do things against her better judgment.

"I suggest the chateaubriand, but the veal is good."

"You've been here before?" With a woman, of course. Who? she wondered and then reminded herself it didn't matter. But she was curious all the same.

"A time or two," he said blandly. He nodded greetings to a couple seated nearby.

"You know, I really don't know much about you," she heard herself saying. And she didn't need to, she warned herself. Tonight would be the last night with him. But her curiosity had taken hold. "Have you ever been married?"

"No."

"Engaged?"

He fingered the edge of his napkin. "Not exactly."

Jacinda wanted to pursue that much further, but she hesitated. The way he was looking at her over the rim of the glass was unsettling. He was smiling faintly and there was a knowing look in his eyes, as if she were a book he had already read. She didn't like being so transparent. She shifted in her chair. "Well, say something."

"What would you like me to say?" he asked amicably.

"Tell me about yourself."

"I was an adorable baby. My mother has tons of photograph albums to prove it. At five months I got my first tooth, and by eight months I had several. Let's see, what else can I tell you . . ." He stared off into the distance reflectively.

She refused to be baited. "Tell me something about your more recent life."

"More recent? Less than an hour ago I was kissing a very beautiful, very unpredictable lady. I intend to resume that later," he added significantly.

She looked away and shook her head. "No. Eric, this is all wrong."

"Then let's make it right." He grasped her hand firmly. "Tell me what it is you want."

She tried to slip her hand from his, but he tightened his grip. "I—it would probably be better if you and I didn't get too deeply involved." She exhaled a deep breath. "In fact, I don't think we should see each other after tonight."

He studied her narrowly, then leaned back in his chair. "That's out of the question. I have to see you again."

Once more she tried to withdraw her hand. "There are lots of very pretty girls in Fayetteville," she pointed out weakly.

"I have to see you."

She frowned at him. Was she imagining it or were his eyes actually twinkling? "Why?" she asked, suspicion beginning to awaken.

He indicated his new jacket. "Because I've invested in a whole new wardrobe that only you can appreciate."

Jacinda felt her determination to remain aloof sliding away. "Oh, you did?" Coy flirtation laced her words.

"Yes, I did. And while I can't say I'm entirely comfortable in them, I'll learn to like them."

"I'm sure you will." A smile teased at the corner of his mouth and she felt her defenses crumbling.

"I also bought a brown argyle sweater. They're in style now," he informed her knowledgeably. "Very trendy on the coasts."

"I see." They both laughed at the same time. "Well, that puts a different light on matters." Her resolve to be reserved was gone. All she could think about was how glad she was to be with him. Freed from having to avoid looking at him, her eyes swept him thirstily. She approved of everything she saw. His hair was much more casual now than it had been when she had opened her door. She liked it better this way. It looked very touchable.

"I thought I'd wear the sweater when we go to the movies," he continued casually. "I know you're dying to see it."

Their hands still lay entwined, but she made no move to draw hers away. "I am." Her smile softened as she continued to gaze at him.

"Good." He turned back to the menu. "Now that we've got that settled, what did you decide you wanted to eat?"

"I'll have the veal." But her mind was on another kind of hunger. She thought of the delicious kisses she and Eric had exchanged in her apartment. Physically he affected her as no man ever had, she considered as she smoothed her fingertips over her napkin. Yes, physically. But that was the problem. Did they have anything beyond the sensual to bind them together? What was Eric really like? Her first impression of him had been that he wasn't particularly intelligent. But his invention surely dispelled that notion. Didn't it? Still, the subjects they could discuss were limited. If she mentioned Oates would he think of Joyce Carol or horses? Would Minoan be a type of tiny fish to him? Had he ever attended a play or the symphony? She doubted it.

"You're awfully quiet," he said.

She smiled faintly. "Thinking."

"Do that some other time. Talk to me now."

"Do you have any hobbies?"

He shrugged. "I suppose you could count my tinkering as a hobby. I don't hunt or anything like that, although I like to go out into the woods sometimes just to be by myself. Lately, I haven't had much free time though. I've been working hard at the quarry."

Further proof that they weren't alike. She'd go crazy alone in the woods. "What about books? Do you read much?"

"Technical manuals, nonfiction, that sort of thing. I'm not much on fiction."

"Oh." She loved a good book.

He cocked his head quizzically. "Why all the questions? Am I being interviewed for a job?"

Jacinda laughed lightly. "Just curious." She was thankful when the waiter arrived and diverted Eric's attention. He was right; she wouldn't ask any more questions. Tonight she wasn't going to think about the differences between them. She was simply going to enjoy herself.

After the waiter left, Eric turned back to her. "Let's talk about you, you seem much more interesting. Any brothers or sisters?"

"A sister who lives in Jersey."

"Your sister lives in a cow?" he asked politely.

"New Jersey—the state," she clarified with a reproving grin. "Her name's Liz. My parents live in New York. Dad's a clinical biologist and Mother's a research librarian."

"Interesting." He finished his wine. "No one in my family has ever graduated from high school."

"Oh." There it was again, that gap between them cropping up even when she didn't want to examine it. But it wasn't something she could ignore.

Two hours later Eric deposited her at her door, and she steeled herself against being swept away by his embrace. Surprisingly he gave her only a chaste kiss, then turned and walked away. She probably should have been grateful. She wasn't.

CHAPTER FIVE

Saturday Philip showed her around the campus. Afterward, they went back to her apartment for a game of chess. Sitting on the floor across from him, Jacinda studied the figures on the board. Philip was an adequate chess player, she decided, but he played by the book, so his moves were a little too obvious. Her own style of playing wasn't so predictable. Sometimes she even surprised herself. But she had a flair for the game and she won far more often then she lost.

"The Met comes to Dallas every year," Philip said. "I think I could get tickets if you'd like to go."

"That might be fun." Strangely, his East Coast accent sounded distinctive, even a little foreign. In the past weeks she'd grown accustomed to the soft Arkansas burr. In fact, she thought she was even picking up a trace of it herself.

"I'll look into it and let you know," he said.

She nodded and moved her knight. "Check."

Within ten minutes she had won the game. Tactfully she put the chess set aside. "Would you like something else to drink?"

"No, I'd better be going." He rose stiffly and reached down to muss her hair. "If you think I'm leaving because I'm a sore loser, you're absolutely right. But tomorrow I intend to take my revenge on the tennis court."

She smiled and uncurled from her yoga position. "Fair enough." She removed his plaid scarf and camel-hair coat from the closet and handed them to him.

Philip took them from her arms, set them back on the sofa, and pulled her against him. "To the victor belongs the spoils. Since you won, I'm all yours." Pushing back a lock of her hair, he continued, "I could even be coerced into staying the night."

With a light kiss she slipped out of his arms. "I don't want to take advantage of you in a moment of weakness," she parried.

After a long silence he asked, "Can I ask you a question?"

"Yes." But she felt wary.

"Is there someone else? Because I get this feeling you don't want to get too involved with me."

Jacinda stared up at him. He was quite handsome with his pure blue eyes and light brown hair, but he wasn't as nice looking as— Resolutely she slammed the door on that thought. "Philip, I think you and I have a lot in common, and I think we could become very close. I just"—she shrugged helplessly—"I just don't want to rush into anything. That's all."

77

"I guess I can understand that. I don't like it," he added, "but it'll do for now." Smiling, he brushed a kiss over her slightly parted lips. "I feel like I'm not doing them justice," he said ruefully.

With a laugh she turned him toward the door. "Good night, Philip."

"Tennis tomorrow. I'll be by to pick you up at two."

"Right." She remained standing at the door long after he was gone. It was the end of September and the leaves had turned to brilliant reds and golds. She loved this season. Although it would have sounded silly if she'd told anyone, she liked the fact that the leaves were noisy. She could hear them crunch beneath her feet when she walked and when she awoke in the night it calmed her to hear the fallen ones swirling in the autumn winds and rustling on the sidewalks.

While she couldn't say that Arkansas had taken the place of home, she had to admit it was becoming more familiar. So were the people. Her ear was now so in tune to the Ozark accent that she scarcely heard it. And she was growing accustomed to the fact strangers sometimes spoke to her on the street just because they were friendly. Of course, she still missed New York.

At midnight on Monday night Eric was in his workshop refining the details of his latest invention. It was a wind generator that would run on AC rather than DC power and could be built much cheaper than the DC generators. Right now, even the rough spots were ironing out nicely.

Smiling to himself, he closed the notebook and laid it aside. Things were going well at the quarry. Aside from the fact he had a dozen orders, there was the added bonus of finally getting the generator approved. And then there was Jacinda.

His smile grew pensive. He'd had a good time Friday night. And he'd given in gracefully to letting her pay the bill. That night he had done things her way, even going along with this game she was playing of trying to keep him at a distance. But he wasn't going to go along with it indefinitely.

He thought he had a clear idea of what was going through her mind. She didn't want to get mixed up with an Arkansas hillbilly. She was an educated lady who intended to return to New York the first minute she could. But he'd glimpsed moments when she seemed to forget what state she was from, forgot where her degree was from, forgot everything except that they were together.

He liked her most when she was like that. Then she leaned forward with unrestrained interest and her eyes sparkled. He didn't give a damn about all the external differences between them. He wanted to get to know her better and that was what he intended to do. Jacinda North didn't know it yet, but she was about to be the object of a blitz of pure Arkansas charm.

* * *

Jacinda had just returned from lunch Thursday afternoon when Lann strolled through the open door of her office. "The work crew is going out to Eric Fortner's quarry today to set things up. I think it'd be a good idea if you drove out there—just to make sure everything goes without a hitch."

"Fine," she agreed readily. She hadn't seen Eric since the night they had gone out to dinner five days before. Suddenly she was very anxious to remedy that. Without her willing it, a memory of his kisses flashed into her mind with the intensity of sun sparkling on water.

"Don't bother trying to make it back to work today," Lann added.

Nodding, she looked at her rust dress with ivory piping and her high brown heels—hardly the proper attire for a rock quarry. "I think I'll run home and change first."

"Okay. See you in the morning."

Butterflies began to flit in her stomach as she drove to her apartment and changed into a pair of gray corduroy slacks and a charcoal gray sweater. As she pulled on a pair of gaucho boots, she could feel anticipation building like a carefully stoked fire. She longed to see Eric again, even if only on business.

During the drive to the quarry she tried to analyze her barely contained enthusiasm. She hadn't felt this way since she was thirteen and had waited outside school every day to catch a glimpse of Miles Johnston. But that had been only a schoolgirl's infatuation. Thoughtfully she frowned. Was that what her attraction was for Eric—simply infatuation? Or was his appeal the fact he was so different from all the other men she'd ever dated?

In fact, Eric was different from every man she had known since childhood. Her father's friends were professional men who attended plays and argued over the political situation. She couldn't imagine Eric doing that.

Her thoughts turned to all the reasons she and Eric were unsuited for each other, and she knew she ought to be fighting harder to quell her attraction. But today, Jacinda argued stubbornly, she was seeing him for business reasons. She deliberately didn't dwell on the fact she was desperately happy to have that as her excuse.

After following the same rollercoaster road she had taken to Eric's house, she hung a sharp right and followed a dirt road for two miles. It came to a dead end at the quarry. She parked in front of the small stone office building, got out, and looked around. Two bulldozers and a front-end loader steamed around on top of a high hill that had been stripped of trees. A long conveyor ran down the side of the hill. Her eyes were pulled from the work in progress back toward the building. Eric would be inside, she knew. Pulse fluttering, she went in.

Eric was the only person in the one-room office. It was furnished with battered bookcases, metal file cabinets, and two desks. Eric was sitting in front of an ancient typewriter peering down at the keys. He hadn't heard her enter, she realized, and she waited quietly, smiling as she watched him. His index fingers were pointed at the keys like loaded pistols.

"Where in hell is the 'd'?" he muttered to himself. She giggled.

Looking up, he saw her and his eyes lit with pleasure. "Hello. This is an unexpected treat."

She felt warmed by his smile, and for a moment she forgot why she'd come. Then it dawned on her that the silence was lengthening while they gazed at each other. "Our crew is coming today to get everything lined out for the conveyor system. I came to make sure there aren't any problems."

"I appreciate that." He turned back to the typewriter. "Let me finish this letter and I'll be right with you."

Smothering a smile, she sat down in a leather chair. She didn't think he'd be *right* with her. At the rate he typed, it could be several months, but she didn't mind waiting. She liked the way he looked with his mouth set in a determined line, his eyes scanning the keys for the appropriate letter. Finally he pulled the sheet from the typewriter with a grand flourish.

"Don't you have a secretary?" she asked.

"Part-time. She comes in in the mornings and does the books and typing. But I needed to get this out right away. One of the men will mail it tonight in town."

Through a nearby window she saw a power company truck pull up and was disappointed that they'd arrived so soon. Having Eric to herself for a little while longer would have been nice.

"Looks like they're here," he observed. His expression told her he, too, wished they hadn't been so prompt.

Rising, she started for the door. "Coming?"

He shook his head regretfully. "I'm busy now, but I'll try to get down there later."

"All right." As she left the office she tried not to think about how much she would have liked to stay with him. Throughout the rest of the afternoon, as the crew set up the necessary equipment, her eyes wandered frequently back toward the office. Eric never joined them. At five o'clock she walked back toward her car.

Eric was just locking the door when she reached the office. "Sorry I didn't get down there to watch. I've been tied up on the phone. Everything okay?"

"Fine."

"Since you're here, why don't you come by my house for dinner?" he suggested easily. "Nothing fancy, of course."

Her first reaction was delight. She was on the brink of saying yes when a more practical voice intruded. An evening alone with Eric wouldn't be wise, it cautioned, especially in view of the spark that always ignited when they were together. On the other hand, a more daring, eager voice countered. She *was* here and it would seem rude to say no. Jacinda was much more inclined to listen to the latter voice. "Sounds good."

He smiled and got into his truck. "Follow me."

Jacinda followed the cloud of dust left behind as he drove down the dirt lane to its intersection with the gravel road. Minutes later they were at his house. He put her to work in the kitchen making a salad while he left to take a shower.

Ten minutes later he was back wearing clean jeans and a a green plaid shirt. His hair was still damp and a drop of water glistened above one eyebrow. Even his lips looked dewy and inviting. She forced herself to look away.

"How about hamburger?" he asked.

"Sounds great." As he brushed past her, she smelled soap and a pleasant whiff of lime. It wasn't easy to be in Eric's presence and ignore the sensual effect he had on her. But she didn't regret coming here tonight; she had wanted desperately to be with him.

He began frying the hamburgers and she set catsup and mustard on the table in the adjoining dining area. While she was putting pickles on the table, she noticed a chess set in the corner. "Do you play chess?" she asked when he arrived with the sandwiches.

He glanced at the board disinterestedly. "Not really. I just learned a couple of weeks ago."

"Oh." Then she definitely didn't want to challenge him. With her experience, he wouldn't be a match for her, and she didn't want to crush his ego by beating him.

"Help yourself to the potato chips," he invited.

Throughout the meal they carried on a desultory conversation. Afterward, Jacinda was helping clear the table when she brushed against his arm. He winced and drew back.

She was so stunned, the dishes nearly slid from her hands. "What's wrong?"

"Just have a slight cut; nothing to worry about." He disappeared into the kitchen.

Jacinda followed. "Let me see."

"It's nothing. Would you like to watch television?"

"No, I want to see your arm," she pursued stubbornly.

Wordlessly he rolled up his sleeve.

"My heavens!" He had skinned it from his elbow to his wrist. Several deeper purple gashes slashed across the raw flesh. Her eyes flew to his face. "What happened?"

He shrugged. "I was helping my father put up fence on his farm last weekend. I had an argument with a roll of barbed wire and lost."

She clucked her tongue in disapproval. "Why haven't you put anything on it?"

"I had something on, but it came off in the shower. I'll see about it later," he finished indifferently.

"We'll see about it *now*. Come with me." Marching into the bathroom, she began pulling items out of the medicine cabinet. "Don't you know it could get infected?" she lectured severely.

"Yes, ma'am."

"You should have seen a doctor."

"Yes, ma'am."

"Take off your shirt."

"*Yes*, ma'am."

She ignored his suggestive smile as he began shrugging out of his shirt. She reached toward him. "I'll help."

"Better and better."

Gingerly she eased the sleeve over the raw area, then uncapped the iodine. "This is going to sting a bit."

"It's going to hurt like hell," he contradicted, and drew in a sharp breath as she applied it.

She looked sympathetically into the pain-narrowed brown eyes. "How are you doing?"

His smile was wan. "I've already bitten the bullet in two if that's what you mean."

"Just let me cover it." Carefully she applied a bandage. "There, that's much better." She began rolling the shirt sleeve down over the bandage. Without looking up, she knew he was watching her. There was something intimate about caring for another's

86

wounds, and she sensed a subtle change in the atmosphere between them.

"Thank you," he said quietly.

Jacinda looked up then. His hair was almost dry now and she could see individual strands of gold layered in with the downy blond. His bottom lip curved into that familiar, warmly seductive smile. Slowly, as if she had no control over her own hand, she reached up and traced the outline of his lips.

Their kiss was as inevitable as rain in spring. And as gentle. She felt protective toward him, and took care not to press against his arm as his mouth passed lightly over hers. Then he kissed her cheeks, the bridge of her nose, her chin, and finally burrowed against her neck.

Jacinda stroked her hands through the soft down of his hair. It was happening again; she was being drawn into his spell. She knew that, and she didn't want it to stop. His left arm hung limply at his side while he pulled her closer with his right.

He rained kisses at the base of her throat, and she felt her pulse begin to quicken beneath the demands of his mouth. Her back was against the wall now, and his body held her there while he slid a hand beneath her sweater. His fingers tingled on the bare skin as they trailed slowly upward toward her lacy bra. Finally he reached the soft fullness of her breast and her breathing thickened as she felt his warm, work-roughened palm cupping her breast. His mouth moved down her neck, trailing a smoky fire, and a kaleidoscope of sensations pulsed through her.

Slowly he lifted his head. For an endless moment they looked at each other in silence. Words were pointless. His eyes told her how much he wanted her, and hers gave back the same answer.

Taking her hand, he led her through the living room. It was dusk now and the interior of the house was shrouded in darkness. But he was in familiar territory and guided her unerringly into the bedroom.

Jacinda undressed herself, letting her clothes rustle to the floor. Then she helped him ease his shirt off his tender arm. Together they lay between the cool, satiny sheets and reached for each other. She touched his arm reverently. "I'll be careful."

He chuckled. "That's my line."

He began with slow, anointing kisses on her forehead and gradually moved down to her mouth. He took his time, feathering easy kisses on her cheeks, even on her eyelids. By the time his lips reached hers, she was grievously hungry for the taste of them. Their mouths met and clung in a searing burst of passion. She felt his hands sculpting over the fullness of her breasts, then learning them more fully with a massaging touch. She let her own hands wander, exploring the curve of his hips and the corded muscles on his back.

Lifting her closer against him, he pressed her down into the mattress as his mouth moved deeper into the intimate territory of hers. Her fingers curled around his shoulders as she struggled to return each intense caress. He was strong and demanding and his touch was sure. Very sure. When his hands moved lower and traced hidden secrets, she felt her control ebbing away. She wanted him. Now.

But he continued to tease and cajole and drug her with promising, passionate kisses. When she could stand it no longer, she fought her mouth away from his. "Eric, I want—"

He captured her lips again while his hands returned to touch the swollen, aching tips of her breasts. She thought she would die from wanting. Finally he slipped inside her. For a moment she was conscious only of relief. Then he began to move against her and the burning waves of desire built again, higher and faster and spinning out of control. She felt like a swimmer being lashed by a storm and all she could do was hold on.

When he lifted her hips and arched her closer to him, she felt the first drops of pure pleasure flow through her. They invaded her blood with each movement he made and reached farther toward the center of her being. His mouth still covered hers and his satiny tongue was as much a part of her being as her own. In fact, she didn't know where she left off and he began. All she knew was that she was moving toward a peak of pleasure and she strained toward it desperately. Then all at once they reached it together. Bright colors flashed and someone cried out and then they were both still.

Damp and exhausted, her breathing still coming in erratic breaths, she fell asleep in Eric's arms.

CHAPTER SIX

It was early in the morning when Jacinda awoke. For a moment she was disoriented. Then she felt a hand on her thigh, and every detail came back to her. Turning over, she fitted herself against the curve of Eric's back, smiling like a contented kitten.

"Is that you, Gertrude?"

For an answer she swatted his rear.

"Ah, it is you." He rolled over and dragged her against him.

She planted a dewy kiss on his chest before lifting her head to his mouth. At the same time her playful hands sought his ribs and she tickled him gleefully.

Clamping her arms to her sides, he held her away from him. "First you come down here with your flashy city ways and high button shoes and take advantage of a poor country boy, and now you want to play rough with me." His smile was mischievous.

"Yeah, I do," she agreed readily. She loved that smile. It made her feel very young and carefree. It also made her glow with memories of last night. He

91

had been a sensitive and passionate lover, giving as well as demanding, and she was anxious to experience it all again.

Eric smoothed her tangled hair back and kissed the top of her head. "Ready for breakfast?"

"Do we have to get up so soon? I had other plans. . . ." She trailed off suggestively.

"You can go blind from that, you know," he reproved her, and sat up on the side of the bed, reaching for his boots.

Jacinda rose, too, and put her arms around his neck, smiling as she leaned against his smooth back. "I don't mind. How's your arm feeling this morning?"

Turning, he pulled her onto his lap. "Fine, I'd love to show you just how fine," he whispered against her hair, "but I've got to be at the quarry this morning for a little while."

"Oh." She was sharply disappointed.

"Wait for me here. I'll be back around ten and we can spend the rest of the day together."

Jacinda nodded and he set her on the bed again.

"Sleep awhile longer if you like. Make yourself at home." He was buttoning his shirt now and tucking it into his jeans.

"What about breakfast?"

"I probably don't have time. You'll find everything you need in the kitchen."

He started from the room, then turned back and

wrapped her close against him. For a moment he held her wordlessly, then he released her and left.

Jacinda lay on the bed for a long time after he had left, thinking about that hug and about last night. She deliberately didn't consider anything else. Today she didn't care that she and Eric were all wrong for each other. She simply intended to savor the wonder of being with him.

She only wished he were holding her. Of course, she ought to appreciate his dedication to his work. Diligence was a quality she admired. But this morning all she knew was that it had taken her away from him, and away from the lazy, sensuous morning they could have shared. The bed seemed very empty without him.

On that thought she threw back the covers and dressed. Then she padded barefoot into the kitchen, a small, neat room with cabinets of glass and natural oak. After making toast and coffee, she sat down at a small round table and ate, chewing slowly as she looked out the window into the trees. They were half bare now, and while she watched, the wind sang through the trees and more leaves fluttered to the ground. The sound of the wind was the only sound she heard. When it died there was nothing but the silence.

Abruptly, Jacinda rose and busied herself washing her dishes in the stainless steel sink. She clattered the dishes purposely and hummed loudly to herself. Still, she could feel the silence.

"Anybody home?"

She breathed a sigh of relief at the sound of Eric's voice. "In the kitchen."

Eric joined her. He was wearing a brown Windbreaker that was the color of his eyes. "You should have left the dishes. I'd have done them later."

"I didn't mind." She dried her hands on a towel. "How was everything at the quarry?"

"Fine, I got pretty well caught up." He lifted her hair and kissed the nape of her neck. "Mmm, you smell good—clean and fresh, like the woods after a rain. Speaking of the woods"—he paused to brush another kiss on her neck—"I thought I'd show you the great outdoors today. The weather's great; you won't even need a jacket." Taking her hand, he started out the back door.

Jacinda dragged her feet. She would be content to spend the day indoors. Besides, he was going out the back door. "You mean we're not driving?"

"Of course not."

Her reluctance mounted. "Is it warm enough for snakes to be out?" she asked apprehensively.

He laughed and pulled more firmly on her arm. "Come on."

"I hope that means no," she muttered as she followed him. Wooden steps led down to the ground at the back of the house. Trees crept right up to the back of the house, as if to enfold it in the forest beyond.

She glanced around uncertainly. "Any grizzly bears out here?"

Eric hooted, picked her up, and swung her around. "I promise I'll return you to the house safe and sound. Okay?"

His hands still rested on her waist and his eyes sparkled with mirth. At that moment Jacinda knew she couldn't refuse him anything he wanted. Besides, his enthusiasm was infectious. For the first time in her life she felt an urge to explore the silent woods. "Okay."

They started down a thin trail and soon the house had disappeared from sight. As they tramped deeper into the woods, Eric related Arkansas history in bits and pieces. "There used to be a couple of old cabins on the property, but they're gone now. I've heard one of them was on the Butterfield stage route, but I don't know if that's true. The stage did come through Fayetteville though." He was ahead of her, his footsteps sure on the uneven path.

Jacinda followed more carefully. A few minutes later he stopped at the base of a cliff and she paused beside him. Moss and ferns hung from the rock wall and water trickled down the sides, glistening when the sun peeping through the trees touched it.

"That's an artesian spring." He pointed to a pool of clear water half hidden by an overhanging ledge. "The settlers depended heavily on those springs. They built their houses near them. The Indians used them too." Tilting his head back, he pointed upward.

"There's a cave up there I thought we'd go into. It's interesting. Indians lived in it several centuries ago. And before the Second World War men mined zinc from it. When the war started, though, all the mines around here closed and most have never reopened."

Jacinda was only half listening as she stared upward, frowning. "I've never been inside a cave," she began.

He smiled reflectively. "I haven't been in this cave for a while."

"I'm a little claustrophobic," she added as he began to climb.

"The view from the top is great," he called back.

Reluctantly Jacinda began to climb up the rocky cliff that formed a kind of crude stair. But she was full of reservations. What if she or Eric fell? They were so far from a hospital or civilization that it would be impossible to get help. If he were hurt, she wouldn't even know which direction to go to find the closest house.

But Eric was obviously unperturbed by such matters. He scaled up the cliff with agile strength. Jacinda pursued more laboriously. Once she was above the tops of the smaller trees, she kept her eyes directed upward, refusing to look down.

By the time Eric pulled her up to a wide ledge, she was panting heavily. "Here it is." He pointed proudly toward a large opening in the rock face.

Jacinda ventured closer and peered into the blackness. "We can't go in *there*. We don't have a flashlight." *Thank God.*

He produced one from the pocket of his Windbreaker. "Sure we do. Come on." But when he took her arm, she held back.

"Eric, I don't think I want to go in." The cave opening looked ominous and forbidding. If something happened to them, it'd be years before they were discovered. Vague, unsettling thoughts of some future archaeologist poring over her bones passed through her mind. "I don't like the looks of it."

He smiled at her—that slow, melting smile that played havoc with her logic. "You go into the subways, don't you?"

"Sometimes," she admitted.

His smile deepened. "This is just like a subway only without the graffiti." Picking up a lock of her hair, he wrapped a curl around his finger. "If you really don't want to go in, then we won't. But there's nothing to be afraid of, I promise."

When he talked to her like that, low and soothing, she would believe him if he told her Attila the Hun was a nice, misunderstood guy. She nodded her agreement, still gazing up into his mesmerizing brown eyes.

"Good." He put his arm around her shoulder and drew her close against his body. It felt strong and sinewy and she felt completely protected. "The minute you want to come out we will," he added gravely.

Once they were inside the cave, Jacinda was glad

he had insisted. It wasn't black and spooky as she had expected. In fact, the walls of the cave glittered with sparkling crystals. Jacinda thought it was like discovering a fairy's house, and she marveled that a place of such wonder existed quietly, hidden in the empty woods.

"What are those crystals?" she asked in awe.

"Quartz and sphalerite and probably galena," he explained. "Here's some of the old mining equipment." The flashlight was directed toward a set of narrow, rusty tracks that led off into the darkness. A cart still sat on the tracks. "There used to be some Indian pictographs farther back, but they've been pretty well destroyed."

Jacinda could hear regret and wistfulness in his voice. She was so close to him, she had to look straight up to see his expression. The glow of the flashlight accented the lines and planes of his face, emphasizing his slight smile. Suddenly she felt very, very good. Smiling to herself, she pressed closer against him and looked with wonder at the sparkling walls.

They explored for another fifteen minutes before they started out. "Now, which way is the entrance?" he wondered aloud.

She smiled serenely. She could already see the light from the cave mouth.

Stepping out of the cave onto the wide ledge, she saw the view for the first time. They were well above the treetops and the panorama stretched endlessly.

Blue skies formed a canopy for the red and gold treetops. In the distance she saw a flash of silver where a creek purled, and far away smoke curled into the sky, the only hint of human habitation.

"Peaceful, isn't it?" he asked quietly.

"Yes," she murmured. It was hard to believe such solitude existed on the same planet as Fifth Avenue. At that moment New York and its constant stream of people didn't seem quite real. "You can really get caught up in the spell of the woods, can't you?"

He nodded his agreement silently and took her hand as they started down the cliff. This time Jacinda didn't even think about the danger of falling.

Once they were back in the woods, they stopped to watch a darting hummingbird and then to examine animal tracks left in the soft dirt. "Buck," Eric pronounced. "Going down to the creek."

"I'd like to see the creek."

They followed the tracks to a clear, rippling stream. Beside it, Jacinda sat down and wrapped her arms around her knees, throwing her head back to let the sun warm her face. It felt deliciously soothing. "I don't think I'm ever going to get up."

"Oh, yes, you are," he chuckled. "I'm not going to carry you all the way back to the house."

Through half open eyelids she slanted a look up at Eric. He was standing beside the water with his back to her and his hands fitted on his hips. His legs were spread in a way that revealed the muscular taper of his thighs. The sun played in his hair. Jacinda thought he looked completely male, completely seductive. It was impossible not to think of last night.

He turned then, picked up a handful of sand and gravel and dropped down beside her. "Look at this."

Opening her eyes fully, she stared down at his hands. He sorted through the gravel in one palm with his index finger. He was showing her the bits of rock, but her gaze was on the big, callused hand. Until last night no one with work-hardened hands had ever touched her. She had always dated professional men with smooth hands and manicured nails. But none whose touch had been as exciting as Eric's.

"These fragments are quartzes and granite," he informed her. "They come from rocks hundreds, maybe thousands of miles away. They washed down glacial rivers and were deposited when the current slowed," he concluded absently, continuing to sort through the bits of minerals.

Her mind wasn't on rocks at all. Instead, her gaze trailed from his hands up to the bandage showing below the cuff of his Windbreaker. "How's your arm?" She touched it gently.

He looked at her, grinned, then kissed her hard on the mouth. "I can see you're not interested in my natural history lessons."

"Yes, I am," she protested even as she hoped he would kiss her again.

He didn't. Instead, he leaned back on his elbows and nodded toward the opposite bank. "There's buried treasure along here somewhere."

She leaned back beside him. "How do you know?"

"My mother's great-grandfather cleared this land. He buried what little silver and jewels they had once, before an Indian raid. Afterward, he never could find it." Eric smiled pensively. "You wouldn't believe the amount of time I spent down here digging when I was a kid."

A picture focused in her mind of Eric as an angelic, blond-haired little boy industriously burrowing into the ground. The image was endearing and made her feel very close to him.

"I never found anything," he concluded. For several minutes they laid side by side without speaking. Then he leaned over to whisper in her ear.

"I beg your pardon!" But his suggestion was already stirring her blood and fresh memories of last night surfaced. Perversely, though, Jacinda changed the subject to something that had nagged at the back of her mind since Friday. "At the restaurant when I asked you if you'd ever been engaged, you said sort of. What does that mean?"

Lazing back on his elbows again, he squinted up at the sky. "Her name was Laura. She was a wonderful girl."

Already Jacinda didn't like her.

"We'd known each other all our lives. We even lived together for a few months about four years ago. But things didn't work out," he finished.

"Why not?" She scooped up some sand and tried to act casual as she let it trail through her fingers.

"I don't know. I was having a hard time making ends meet at that time. I was trying to get a business off the ground and it wasn't going anywhere. It eventually failed." He flung a handful of gravel to the ground as if his anger at that failure was still fresh in his mind.

She blinked. "But your parents have money. Couldn't they have helped you?" After all, he was their only son and it would all be his someday anyway.

Eric looked at her sharply. "I want to succeed on my own. And I had a good plan," he added in a subdued voice. "It was a hydroponics system, but it was ahead of its time. None of the nurseries would touch it then; now a lot of them are installing systems like it. Anyway," he said after a long pause, "I didn't have much money and I was spending all my time trying to get my system off the ground and it eventually put too much of a strain on our relationship."

"You mean it was the right person but the wrong time?" Her nerves felt raw talking about this mysterious Laura, but Jacinda was unwilling to drop the conversation.

"I didn't say that," he responded slowly.

"Where is she now?"

"In Little Rock. She's married and has a kid." He moved suddenly, stretching out above her as he pushed her flat to the ground. "If you're trying to find out if I still love her, I don't. Do you know that you have beautiful eyes?" His kiss was long and languorous, inviting a response she couldn't deny.

"But you still feel something for her, don't you?" she asked when she caught her breath.

"No. Will you shut up while I'm trying to seduce you?"

Meekly she complied, fitting herself tightly against him and answering his lengthening kiss. They were both breathless when he raised his head. "Let's go back to the house." Rising, he pulling her up after him. Slowly he ran his hands over her to dust the sand from her back. His hands lingered on her bottom, smoothing his hands around in a sensuous circle. "Very nice—for a city woman," he added, the dimple coming into play.

She sniffed haughtily.

Hand in hand they started back.

At the house they clamored up the wooden steps together and he drew her toward the bedroom. "You're a sex fiend," she murmured as he laid down beside her.

"Any objections?"

"No, just an observation."

He took her clothes off slowly, as if she were a present that had been delivered by surprise and whose unwrapping he wanted to savor. When she was completely undressed, he unleashed a torrent of kisses on her bare skin. Closing her eyes, she ran cupped fingers through his hair.

She felt the same swift arousal, the same exquisite

103

fulfillment she had known last night. Only this time it was all the sweeter for being familiar.

Afterward, they lay nestled in each other's arms.

Sunday night Jacinda floated back into her apartment. All the way back from Eric's, she had giggled for no reason at all. And it had been difficult to concentrate on her driving. Something Eric had said would pop into her mind and she would laugh aloud. She felt as if she carried a great secret within and that she would burst if she didn't talk to someone and tell about the magnificent time she and Eric had shared.

She wanted to call every one of her friends in New York. She wanted to call her sister, Liz. She wanted to climb up onto her apartment roof and shout to the world how wonderful she felt. But when she finally picked up the phone and dialed, it was her parents' number.

"Hello, Mom, it's Jacinda." Her excitement was barely restrained.

"How are you, dear! Henry, it's Jacinda. Get on the other phone."

Her father picked up the extension a moment later. "Hi, kid, how's everything?"

"Just fine. In fact, fabulous! I've met a terrific man and—"

"Yes, you told us," her mother cut in. "Philip. He sounds charming. And it's nice that he may get a position at Columbia."

Jacinda picked up the phone and carried it around

he living room, too stimulated to sit in one spot. "This is another man. He's from Arkansas."

"What does he do?" her father asked.

"He runs a quarry," she answered, impatient to tell about the more pertinent things—like his irresistible personality and laid-back charm.

"Is he a mining engineer?" her father pursued.

"No."

"Geologist?"

"Henry," her mother put in, "give the girl a chance to tell us about him."

"He doesn't have a degree, Dad. He didn't even finish high school." But that didn't matter. What mattered was that being with him was like living in a dream.

There was a moment of silence before her mother began, "Well, I'm sure he's very nice—"

Her father interrupted. "Isn't it rather unusual for a girl with a master's in engineering to date a high school dropout?"

"Hen—ry." His wife drew the word out reprovingly.

He ignored her. "I don't mean to interfere, Jacinda, but I am curious."

"He's intelligent enough, and we get along well." She felt suddenly defensive and she didn't want to feel that way. What she wanted was for them to understand how intoxicated Eric made her feel.

"I'm sure you do," her mother agreed staunchly.

"And she's old enough to run her own life, Henry," she added significantly.

"I'm not trying to run her life," he grumbled. "Can't a man ask his own daughter a few innocent questions? Just seems a little strange the kind of guy she's seeing, that's all."

"The weather's been gorgeous here, dear," her mother noted cheerfully.

Her father was undeterred. "I remember how upset she got the last time over that Tony fellow. I just don't want to see her get mixed up with the wrong guy again."

"We're having good weather here, too, Mother." But it was impossible to ignore her father's words.

"What about that other guy—Philip? You still seeing him?"

"Yes, Dad."

"Well, I just think you might have more in common with him."

Her mother joined in again. "Liz just left a few minutes ago. She's moving back to the city, so you two girls will be able to see each other more when you get back."

"That will be lovely," she said absently.

She wished she hadn't told them about Eric. Her father's questions were the exact ones she had been trying to avoid. All the uncertainties she had attempted to push from her mind came flooding back.

That night Jacinda had trouble sleeping. When she finally did, her dreams were painful ones about Tony.

106

She relived the agonizing scene when she had told him she couldn't marry him, and she felt again all the pain of loving a man with whom there could be no future. The next morning she awoke feeling depressed, and her thoughts were centered on inevitable partings and overwhelming barriers.

If she let things continue as they were with Eric, perhaps her attraction for him would run its course and fade. But what if it didn't? What if it became even stronger? How would she cope when the time came to return to New York? Eric had a life here; she couldn't imagine him living in the city, yet that was where her world was centered.

The weekend had been fabulous, but her relationship with Eric couldn't last. And it was better to end it before they became even more deeply involved. Somehow, she had to find the resolve to stop seeing him.

CHAPTER SEVEN

Early Monday morning Eric stood outside his office staring off into the hills in the distance. A slight smile played on his face at the memory of how fascinated Jacinda had been by the cave. It made him want to show her other little-known aspects of the Ozarks. He was glad there would be plenty of time for that.

Watching Jacinda open up to him was like seeing a sunflower blossoming and turning its face toward the sky. She no longer bore any resemblance to the reserved and distant woman he'd first met. Whatever her reservations had been about him in the beginning, she was obviously over them now.

He was glad of that. The more he saw of Jacinda, the more he liked her. He wanted to know her much better. And he wanted her to know him better too.

Monday morning Jacinda was staring abstractedly down at a memo when Lann walked into her office. He stopped in front of her desk and fingered a brass paperweight with his pudgy fingers. "Are you going to be busy Friday night?"

"Nothing definite." She smiled. "Another school carnival?"

"No, this is a party for the people who worked at the first one. Masie's giving it. It'll be a potluck dinner. And bring a date." He wriggled his eyebrows in a terrible impersonation of Groucho Marx. "Masie suggested a certain tall man who runs a quarry and who shall remain nameless. His initials are E.F.," he threw in helpfully.

"I—" She broke off and bit her lip uncertainly, wavering in her determination not to see him. Just one more time couldn't hurt, she argued with herself. But it could hurt. Already her attraction for him was almost out of hand. The only way she could control it was not to see him again.

Lann watched her curiously. "Of course, you can bring anybody you want." He grinned disarmingly. "I know you're seeing that college teacher. Bring him and I'll explain to Masie that Eric had a broken leg."

"I believe I will bring Philip," she murmured, but she was still fighting back a desire to invite Eric. *Just this once,* a voice within pleaded. But she couldn't give in.

"Fine." He shuffled out of the office.

It hadn't occurred to her that Philip might not want to go to the party. Yet when she called him from her apartment that evening, he sounded unenthused. "Couldn't we just go out by ourselves that night?"

"I've already accepted," she explained. "Why don't you want to go?"

"Jacinda, you know it'll be a bore. I don't mean to sound like a snob, but how much do either of us have in common with a bunch of Arkansas PTA members?"

Shaking her handful of newly painted fingernails to dry them, she argued, "They're nice people."

He sighed. "I'm not saying they're not. I just think we could enjoy ourselves more alone than with them. But if you really want to go, I'll go along."

"I'd rather you didn't if it's going to be such a supreme sacrifice," she returned curtly. Eric wouldn't have objected to going. If only . . .

"Let's not get into an argument over this," he said wearily. "When should I pick you up?"

"Six." At least they were in agreement on one point—there was no reason to start a fight over this.

After he hung up, Jacinda slowly applied another coat of polish to her nails. Philip had been in Arkansas two years, she reflected, yet he still didn't feel at ease with the local people. In fact, he was desperate to return to New York. Would she be like that after two years? Or was she growing used to life in Arkansas?

In small ways Jacinda thought she was. At least she no longer rushed everywhere she went. And there were no subways to catch and nowhere in town that couldn't be reached within fifteen minutes. Last Friday at noon she had walked over to the square and strolled through the herb garden in the center. Although she had enjoyed the peaceful walk, perhaps in two years she'd tire of such diversions.

Would she have tired of Eric by then as well? she wondered. Would those brown eyes and the blond hair have lost all their appeal? Once his unique accent became familiar, would it still seem as charming? She couldn't look into the future, but for now she knew that all those things about Eric did affect her. The only way she could avoid falling completely under his spell was to stay away from him.

She had to remind herself of that when he called and asked her out to dinner. The sound of his voice made her clasp the phone tighter and her throat felt dry when she refused him. The next time she turned him down he would surely ask questions and she wasn't at all sure what she would tell him. Resolutely she tried not to think about that.

Friday evening Philip arrived promptly at six wearing chino trousers and a pinstripe shirt. She wore a blue flowered blouse and casual denim skirt she'd bought last week.

Jacinda and Philip were among the first guests to arrive. Masie greeted them at the door of the two-story frame house. "Come in, dear." She smiled at Philip as Jacinda made the introductions. "Pleased to meet you. Go on into the living room." Accepting the Mexican salad Jacinda had brought, she added, "I'll take this back to the kitchen."

In the living room Jacinda recognized several of the people and smiled at them. Philip looked around uneasily.

A thin woman touched her arm and chuckled. "You're the girl who was at the kissing booth, aren't you?"

Philip's head whipped around to stare at her. "Kissing booth?" he whispered incredulously as she moved to Lann's side.

Even if there'd been time to answer, she doubted that she would have. His shocked expression exasperated her. "Philip, I'd like you to meet my boss, Lann Weston."

Lann grabbed his arm and pumped. "Glad to meet you, Phil. I guess Jacinda's told you about the wild time we had at the carnival." He winked at her conspiratorially. "I understand you teach at the college."

"I'm a professor at the university, yes." Philip's Boston Brahmin accent rang as clearly as a bell in the roomful of easy drawls.

"That's great!" Lann said heartily. "Where are you from, Phil?"

"Boston." He pronounced the name with reverence.

"Really?" Lann's eyes lit. "I have a cousin there. Jess Henderson. He's a longshoreman. I don't suppose you know him?"

Philip smiled faintly. "I'm afraid not."

The evening got progressively worse. A few minutes later Philip was trapped into a conversation with an elderly woman who was slightly deaf, and Jacinda could hear his shouted conversation throughout the room. Afterward, someone spilled punch on him as he sat perched on the arm of a chair eating his buffet dinner. He made only minimal conversation for the rest of the evening and began to cast longing glances toward the door, especially during a conversation on the price of crops.

Jacinda took pity on him and leaned toward him. "Do you want to leave?"

"Whenever you're ready," he said neutrally.

They left shortly after ten. "You didn't enjoy yourself, did you?" she asked as soon as they were in the car.

"It was what I'd expected." He started the engine.

"I shouldn't have made you come. I feel guilty that you had such a miserable time."

He gave her a curious look as they passed beneath a streetlight. "I like being with you, Jacinda. That means I'll go places and do things with you that I might not ordinarily do."

She weighed that as he pulled onto the main street. It was flattering that he would put himself out on her account. On the other hand, it would have been even better if he had enjoyed himself. She didn't want to feel someone was making a sacrifice just to be with her. Rather, she wanted to know that they were having fun right alongside her. "What was it that you didn't like about the party?"

His hands tightened on the steering wheel. "I hate being called Phil and I don't like people clapping me on the shoulder. Do you know I talked about shoats with a man for half an hour before I knew we were discussing hogs? Now, let's drop the discussion," he ended testily.

Jacinda nodded. She hadn't particularly enjoyed the party either. Knowing that Philip was miserable had made that impossible. Had she gone with Eric, she probably would have had a good time. But the other side of that coin was that Philip would blend easily at a party in New York. Eric wouldn't. She repressed a sigh. There it was again, the inescapable fact that she and Eric were from two different worlds.

At her apartment Philip parked the car and they walked to her door in silence. She opened it and turned to find herself inches from his chest. Folding his arms around her, he bent to kiss her. After a brief, answering kiss, she moved away.

"Something to drink?" she suggested.

"No." He grasped her hand again. "Jacinda, we've been seeing each other long enough for me to just lay this on the line. I want to stay with you tonight."

She ran her tongue over her dry lips. It was natural for him to want their relationship to progress. She had been holding it at a chaste kiss long enough to try the patience of the most long-suffering man. And she could read the light of desire in his eyes. Tiredly she ran her hand through her hair. It had all seemed so simple when she had first arrived in Fayetteville. Then she had been convinced something would develop between her and Philip. Now she wasn't so sure. He was a good friend, but being with him didn't send a flood of longing through her. Not the way it did when she was with Eric.

"Jacinda. Did you hear me?"

"Yes." The sound was too low for even her to hear. "I'm sorry, Philip, but I don't think it would work. I like you but I don't feel strongly enough about you to go to bed with you. I wish I did," she added, almost to herself.

"It's all right." He kissed her cheek. "As long as there isn't someone else, I'm willing to try to change your mind."

"Philip, I don't know—"

"Shhh." With a parting kiss, he left.

She listened to the sound of his car driving away, then sank onto the sofa, cupping her head between her palms and staring at the floor. Why couldn't it have been Philip who made her heart race? But it wasn't, and she knew there was nothing she could do to change that. She only hoped time would lessen her desire for the man she did want.

By the end of October cool Halloween winds were stirring the air. It had been two weeks since she had seen Eric. If he had called her, then she hadn't been

115

in. Of course, she hadn't been an easy woman to catch lately. To keep from thinking about Eric she tried to stay busy every night doing something outside her apartment. She attended a home-decorating party with Masie, played tennis, played chess, went to the library and leafed through the current magazines. Nothing worked. Eric continued to fill her thoughts.

Sunday night, after a hard-fought tennis game with Philip, she arrived back at her apartment with her racquet slung over her shoulder. The phone was ringing.

"Hello," she said breathlessly.

"Hi, it's Eric."

"Oh, hello." Tension seeped into her pores, along with a delicious sense of elation.

"I'm in town and thought we might go out for a pizza if you're not busy."

She could have said she was busy, or even that she had company, but that would have only stalled the unavoidable. She gripped the phone tighter. "I'm sorry, Eric, I don't think so."

"Is something wrong?"

Her heart thudded louder as she forced herself to say, "Eric, I've done a lot of thinking over the past few days. I'm fond of you, but we're really not right for each other, and I don't think we should continue dating."

After a moment's silence he asked tersely, "When did you decide this?"

"I've known all along."

"I see," was his cryptic answer. "Listen, I'm at a pay phone booth and someone's waiting to use the phone. Is it all right if I come over to your house and we talk?"

"I don't think—"

"I'll be there in ten minutes."

She heard a click and then the dial tone. "Oh, Eric," she murmured and restlessly pushed her thick hair back. Already she knew what the sight of him was going to do to her. But she mustn't allow him to persuade her she was wrong. Her decision was made and she was going to stick with it in spite of Eric's winsome smile and sensual touch.

A few minutes later she heard a car door slam followed by a pounding on her door that sounded like firemen coming through with hatchets. She opened it warily. "Hello, Eric."

He stepped in and unconsciously she took a step backward. He looked tall and forbidding and there was a set to his jaw that spoke of determination and anger. "Okay, let's get to the bottom of this," he began abruptly.

"Don't you want to sit down?" She gestured vaguely toward the sofa.

For an answer he paced to the window, looked out, and then rounded on her. "Why don't you want to see me again?"

Helplessly she spread her hands toward him. "It wouldn't work. We're from two different worlds."

"Oh?" he said sardonically. "The people in New York don't breathe air and eat food?"

Jacinda sank onto the edge of the sofa. "Please don't make this any more difficult than it already is."

His clenched fists slowly uncurled and he slumped into a chair opposite her. "If it's difficult, then why are you doing it? We both want to see each other again and you know it."

She tried not to look at him. "We're too far apart."

"How?"

Jacinda laced her fingers tightly together and stared down at them. "I don't mean to sound like a snob, but I have a great deal more education than you. Then there's the question of what we enjoy. You like the country and I'm a city person. I like the crowds, the excitement, the feeling of being part of a whole that New York gives me. And I like reading good books and watching a ballet. Eric, don't you see, it could never work?"

The brown eyes probed into her. "Then what was that weekend all about? I thought it was working damn well then."

She gestured at nothing in particular. "It was all physical," she said, not looking at him.

His eyes widened, then narrowed. "Well, thank you for pointing that out to me," he said coldly, "because I was stupid enough to believe we felt something for each other. I thought I'd finally gotten behind that damn wall of reserve you throw up around yourself like a portable moat." He stalked to the door. "It's been great knowing you!"

Her eyes were already filling with tears as he slammed the door behind him. Then she heard him drive off with a grinding of gears and a screeching of tires.

She remained immobile, feeling an ache so deep it numbed her. It was finally over between them, and she should have felt relief. But the tears continued to course down her cheeks, and her heart continued to twist.

CHAPTER EIGHT

Over the next week Jacinda kept ferociously busy. A thousand times she was tempted to pick up the phone and call Eric. A thousand times she stopped herself. But that didn't keep her from missing the sound of his voice or the sight of his smile.

On Monday she had just reached her office when her phone rang. She picked it up as she shrugged out of her down-filled coat. "Hello, Jacinda North speaking."

"This is Dr. Metcalf at Stanford University. I teach electrical engineering and I've heard through the grapevine that Ozark Power is buying electricity generated by a conveyor system. Is that correct?"

She blinked. "Why, yes, it is."

"I'm interested in learning more about this. As it happens, I'll be speaking in Kansas City at the end of this week and I'd like to come to Fayetteville afterward. Would you be available to show me the system?"

Absently Jacinda twisted her finger around the

phone cord. "I'd be glad to, but I believe you'd also need to talk with the man who designed it. I could give you his name and phone number." She flipped open her address book and her eyes rested on the swirling letters of Eric's name. Just looking at his name made something lurch inside of her.

"I hate to impose on you, but would it be possible for you to set up a meeting for me? That way you two can figure out a time that would be best for you. I'll be available all day Friday." When she said nothing, he prompted, "Do you mind?"

"Uh—no." It was flattering to have attracted the interest of a Stanford professor, and Jacinda knew she should be going out of her way to accommodate him. But all she could think about was Eric. How would he respond when she called him? How would she feel?

"Good," he approved. "I really appreciate this, Ms. North. I'll come to the power company office Friday morning. See you then."

"Yes." She sat for a long time listening to the dial tone before it occurred to her to hang up. Slowly she put the receiver on the cradle and stared fixedly down at her desk. The memory she had tried so hard to put from her mind came hurtling back. She thought about the night Eric had led her to his bed and remembered the magic that had occurred between them. Was something that intense, that special, purely a physical communion? Or had it been more? Had it been two people joining together who felt something very deep for each other?

Jacinda pushed her hand limply through her hair and looked back at the phone. Whatever had passed between them and whatever might now stand between them, she had a job to do. And that meant she had to get in touch with Eric.

After she wiped her clammy palms against her skirt she reached for the phone. It rang six unnerving times before Eric answered. "Rock quarry."

"Good morning. This is Jacinda." She felt awkward and knew her voice reflected the strain.

"Hello," he said abruptly.

Her reason for calling was business, she reminded herself, and she couldn't wilt simply because he sounded unfriendly. "A Professor Metcalf from Stanford called me this morning. He's going to be in town on Friday and is interested in seeing your generator. If you're available, I'll bring him out to the rock quarry and you can go over the details with him." She held her breath.

"Friday?"

"Yes."

"Couldn't you explain everything to him?"

That hurt. There was no mistaking the implication he didn't want to see her. "I believe he wants to see the system for himself, but I could give him directions to the quarry." She wet her lips. "I don't have to come out there."

He sighed heavily. "There's no point in avoiding

122

each other. Bring your professor out Friday. I'll be here all day." He hung up.

The following days crept by, giving Jacinda ample time to reflect on Friday. As each day passed, a mixture of apprehension and anticipation swelled within. She couldn't deny that she wanted to see Eric. If only the circumstances of the meeting could be different.

By the time Dr. Metcalf came into her office late Friday morning Jacinda's stomach was churning nervously. He was a tall, thin man with a sharply receding hairline and thick glasses.

After they had introduced themselves, she said briskly, "We might as well go on out to the quarry. I'm sure you're anxious to see the conveyor system."

"Yes." He followed her out of the building and toward the company car. "The truth of the matter is I was hired as a consultant to design the same type of operation at a large dam in California." He smiled sheepishly. "My plan didn't work—too much fluctuation in the current. I want to find out where I went wrong."

"Oh." She pondered the professor's admission as she drove away from Fayetteville and turned down the gravel road. Of course she had known Eric's plan was sophisticated, but for the first time it dawned on her just how sophisticated. It was staggering to realize he had accomplished what this highly educated man had not been able to master.

"Tell me something about Mr. Fortner," Dr. Metcalf said easily. "Does he teach here at the university?"

"No."

"What's his background?"

He was bound to find out from Eric, so she might as well tell him now. It might save embarrassment for all of them later. "He's a high school dropout." Jacinda turned to gauge his reaction.

"Hmmm. Interesting." The professor pointed out the window at the rolling hills. "Very pretty countryside."

Jacinda didn't look at the scenery; her gaze was still glued to the professor. "You don't seem surprised to learn Eric Fortner doesn't have much formal education."

"Should I be? There's a great precedent for 'uneducated' inventors. Henry Ford was one of this country's finest inventors and he never finished high school. The Wright Brothers didn't have much formal education either. Lear never went beyond eighth grade and he didn't do so badly. After all, he developed the Lear jet and navigational aids that include the automatic pilot." Dr. Metcalf nodded sagely. "I'm more impressed with results than initials after a person's name."

Jacinda turned onto the dirt road that led to the quarry, feeling humbled by Dr. Metcalf's words. What he said was true, but she hadn't looked at it that way when Eric had sat in her office that first day. She had thought only about his lack of qualifications.

"Is that the quarry ahead?" the professor asked.

"Yes." Dragging her mind back to the present, she stopped in front of the small office.

He looked around approvingly. "Nice little operation. Is Mr. Fortner in charge of it?"

"Yes." It occurred to her that it wouldn't have made any difference to the professor if Eric were the one driving the front-end loader. "Shall we go inside?" she suggested meekly.

Jacinda smoothed back her hair before following Dr. Metcalf through the door. As they entered, Eric rose from behind his desk. He was wearing jeans and a tan cotton shirt with the sleeves rolled up. His hair looked windblown and suddenly she ached to smooth it. But she couldn't. Why had she let her damn caution get her into this position of standing here so formally? Why hadn't she thrown all her caution to the wind and savored a wild, hungry passion with Eric?

"Eric Fortner? I'm Dr. Metcalf."

"Pleased to meet you, sir." Eric came around to the front of his desk and shook hands. "Hello, Jacinda." He nodded curtly.

"I know I'm imposing on both your and Ms. North's time, but when I heard about your operation I was anxious to see it. I hope I haven't put you to a lot of trouble?"

Eric smiled. "No."

She felt something unclench inside of her at the sight of his smile. She only wished it had been for her.

"Shall we go outside?" Eric suggested.

The three of them left the building together. Jacinda realized the two men had sized each other up and liked what they saw; and that made her feel very left out.

As they crossed a wide, empty area, Eric pointed out different parts of the operation. "It's pretty straightforward," he said. "The rocks are being quarried out of the top of the mountain and come down the side of the steep hill on the conveyor belt. That's the generator halfway down the hillside and, of course, that's the grizzly below it, throwing off the big rocks." At the bottom of the hill, a shaker the size of a house sorted the rocks and dumped them into cone-shaped piles.

They climbed to the generator and Eric began explaining how the conveyor operated. Now and then Dr. Metcalf stopped him to ask a question. Jacinda listened silently, feeling superfluous as she watched Eric unroll the plans and point to something. The wind stirred through his hair and when he pushed it back impatiently she saw the jagged marks on his arm.

"I see you've scraped your arm," the professor said nonchalantly.

"Yes." For the first time Eric's eyes came to rest fully on her face. Without expression he added, "But I've been very careful to make sure it doesn't get infected."

"That's good," the professor said. "Those things

can be nasty when they do." He peered closer at the plans. "Oh, I see what you've done here. . . ."

Unable to look away, Jacinda continued to watch Eric with the hunger of one who has been without nourishment for weeks. The sight of that lean body in worn jeans and faded shirt tugged at her heart, so did the sun touching his hair and highlighting strands of gold.

Dr. Metcalf looked up at her. "Do you agree, Jacinda?"

Pulled her out of her reverie, she stared blankly. "Er—yes. Yes, I do."

Eric began refolding the paper while Dr. Metcalf took off his reading glasses and replaced them in his shirt pocket. "Good. Then we'll finish this discussion over dinner." He checked his watch. "We should be going. I imagine Ms. North needs to get the company car back before quitting time."

Startled, she looked from one man to the other. Dinner! How had she missed that part of the discussion? Her eyes flew to Eric and she searched for some sign. Did he want her to go? Even if he did, how was she going to survive an evening trying not to look into those clear brown eyes? His presence would awaken even more of the memories she had tried to lull to sleep.

"I'll pick both of you up this evening," Eric said quietly. "Is seven o'clock all right, Jacinda?"

She nodded mutely. He had whispered her name

127

that night in his bed. Hearing it again sounded like the caress of haunting music.

Dr. Metcalf started toward the car and Jacinda had no choice but to follow. Not that there was any reason she should have remained with Eric, she told herself. But suddenly she was reluctant to leave him.

During the long drive back it was difficult for Jacinda to concentrate on what Dr. Metcalf was saying. She was totally immersed in thoughts about Eric. Already she had endured long days of wanting to call him and refusing to let herself. But she didn't know if she could endure sitting across from him for an entire evening, especially when her feelings were in such tumult. How did he feel right now? He had seemed so cool and distant at the quarry. Tonight was bound to be awkward for both of them.

An hour later she was back at her apartment. With nerveless fingers she dressed in a plum knit two-piece dress and plum stockings, then put on rose lipstick and combed her cloud of dark hair. Just as she was adding a pair of tiny sapphire earrings, the doorbell sounded.

Momentarily she froze. Then she forced herself to pat a tissue to her glistening lips and walk to the door. Her heart thumped so loudly, she was sure Eric must be able to hear it even before she opened the door. When she did open the door, she saw that Eric was wearing the camel suit and her mind went back to the first time he had worn it.

"Hello, Jacinda," he said formally.

He stood rigidly and she knew he saw the whole evening as an ordeal. "Hello, Eric." She picked up her white chenille jacket. "I'm ready," she said brightly and breezed out the door. He followed and held the car door for her.

Silently he drove toward the motel, never taking his eyes off the road or looking at her. It was going to be a long night, she realized.

They were halfway to the motel before she spoke. "I know we're uncomfortable with each other," she finally said, "but I hope we can act cordial around the professor." She glanced at him uncertainly. "Can't we?"

"Whatever you say," he answered remotely.

"Eric, please." She touched his sleeve in a pleading gesture. "Just for this evening. I know how you must feel toward me, but we only have to be civil a few hours."

He stared at her. "How I must feel about you?" he repeated coldly, then turned his attention back to the road. "I don't know how I ever got mixed up with anyone as crazy as you."

She sank lower in the seat. It was going to be a very long evening.

Neither spoke the rest of the way to the motel. But after he parked the car, he turned to her and slowly extended his hand, touching her bottom lip with his thumb. "Your lipstick's a little smeared. I noticed it when I picked you up."

Jacinda watched him uncomprehendingly, then

took out her small lighted compact and lipstick. She didn't understand this man at all. She hadn't thought he'd even looked at her at her apartment, and it surprised her that he cared how she looked.

"I'll do it." Removing the lipstick from her fingers, he smoothed the rich gloss over her upper lip. Moving closer, he began applying it to the bottom lip in a slow, sensuous trail.

Jacinda wanted to say something light and sparkling but could only gaze up at him, trying to read the expression on his shadowed face. Touching her lips was such a simple act to have aroused such a burning need. But it had. She dropped her lashes. "Do I look all right now?"

"Yes. Your hair is in place, your lipstick is on right, and your clothes are straight." He slid even closer and laughed softly. "So why do I want to muss you?"

Without regard for her fresh lipstick, she lifted her mouth to his. It was an instinctive reaction, like a drowning person struggling toward the surface. She didn't even stop to consider whether it was right or wrong as his arms came around her like iron bands and their lips meshed in a fierce embrace. She shivered at the delicious feel of the warm tip of his tongue crossing into her mouth.

"I've been thinking about the reasons you gave for not wanting to see me," he said when he lifted his head. "Maybe they're all true. But there are some other things that are true too. Like the way you looked at me this afternoon when you came into the office. I like being with you," he continued softly. "But I don't want to force you into anything."

She studied him in the dim interior of the car. What was he saying? Suddenly, irrationally, she found herself praying he would knock down all her arguments for not seeing him.

"On the other hand," he continued, "if you could just forget your uncertainties for a while, I think we could have something special. I'm not asking for forever; I know you won't be here forever."

Jacinda rested her cheek against the soft wool of the jacket. She wanted to forget the differences between them, too, but she was practical in spite of the fact she didn't really want to be in this instance. "Eric, we could both end up getting hurt."

"I'm willing to take the chance. It would be a nice memory for a country boy after you're gone." He tilted her chin up so that she was looking into his face. His smile would have been difficult to resist even if she'd wanted to.

"It would be a nice memory for a city girl too," she murmured. As he bent lower, her eyelashes touched his cheek. Why should she deny what they both wanted? At least they could have each other for a while. And it wouldn't be unfair to either of them since they both realized their relationship would end when she returned to New York.

As if he had read her thoughts, he smiled. "Then it's settled."

131

She lifted her chin to a regal angle. "All except your apology for calling me crazy." It felt good to tease with him again. It also felt good to feel his strong arms around her.

He chuckled. "You are crazy, but I think a little more of this country air will clear your head, and I can get you on the right track."

When his lips repossessed hers, their kiss flared to a new level of intensity and Jacinda was willing to agree to everything he said.

Slowly he drew away and brushed her disheveled hair back. "I think we'd better get the good doctor before my thoughts go any further astray." He reached into his pocket and pulled out a handkerchief for her. She blotted her lips with it while he straightened her jacket. "There, you don't look too bad. We'll tell Dr. Metcalf you dressed while fleeing from a fire."

Making a wry face at him, she pulled a comb from her purse. "You just go get him. I'll put myself in order."

"Yes, ma'am." He touched her cheek and left.

As she swept the comb through her hair, she watched him stride to the motel door and knock. He had left her only a moment ago and he would be back in yet another moment but already she ached to have him beside her. The time since they had been together had been long—far too long.

The door opened and Dr. Metcalf stood silhouetted against the lighted room. Then he walked to the car with Eric.

"Hello, Jacinda." He got into the front seat beside her and she moved next to Eric. Their thighs touched and when Eric brushed the side of her breast as he put his right hand on the steering wheel, a sensation like butterflies dancing coursed through her and she edged even closer against him.

By the time they reached the restaurant, Jacinda had surrendered any lingering thoughts of trying to resist the magical pull Eric had on her. She had never believed in brief affairs before—ones that were solely for the moment without thought of the future. But tonight she wanted to be with Eric more than she'd ever wanted anything in her life. For a while she was going to immerse herself in the pleasure of being with him. He was right; it would be a lovely memory to take back to New York.

CHAPTER NINE

They went to the same restaurant Eric had taken her to before. Once there, Jacinda willed herself to keep her attention focused on Dr. Metcalf, although it did wander when Eric's leg accidentally brushed hers. Provocatively she touched his knee.

"Have you ever written a paper before, Eric?" the professor asked.

"No, sir."

"I think you should consider it. What you've accomplished is of great interest to the engineering field. Alternate energy is a very big consideration in our country right now. I assume you've applied for a patent," he said as an afterthought.

"Yes, sir."

"Smart. Now, about this paper, I'd be glad to collaborate on it with you."

"I'm rather busy right now, sir. Besides, I'm not sure I'd know all the correct terms," Eric said.

"I'm sure Ms. North would be glad to help you." The older man smiled at her.

Nodding, Jacinda looked from the professor to Eric. She wondered if Eric realized that Dr. Metcalf's offer to collaborate was really a guarantee that the paper would be published and receive recognition. The prestige of a Stanford professor's name would mean a lot to the editor of a professional journal. "I think it's a very good idea, Eric."

Eric tapped his fingers on the table. "I'll think about it."

"Do," Dr. Metcalf said. "And let me know."

The subject turned to other matters, and Jacinda found her own thoughts straying even further. What was going to happen tonight when Eric took her home? Looking at him now, with his hair gleaming a soft gold in the candlelight and his eyes a warm brown, she felt weak and reckless. Was it insanity to let herself become even more deeply involved with this man, or was it fate? Then he smiled at her—that intimate, promising smile of his—and she felt herself melt.

"Well, I've certainly enjoyed the evening," Dr. Metcalf said an hour later as he pushed back his chair and rose.

The three of them walked to the car together and again she sat beside Eric. Even after they had dropped the professor at the motel, Jacinda remained seated in the middle of the car.

When they reached her apartment, she turned to him. "Like to come in?"

"That depends, what did you have in mind?"

She lifted her chin daintily. "Nothing sinful, I assure you."

"Then I definitely don't want to come in."

Pulling him out of the car, she led him into her apartment. "Dr. Metcalf seems like a nice man. He likes you."

Eric loosened his tie and took off his jacket. "I know. He kept fondling my knee all evening."

"That was me," she said sweetly.

"Oh, well, then I'll bet he thinks it strange that I fondled his knee back." He sat down on the sofa and stretched a hand toward her. "Why don't you come here and whisper your fantasies into my ear and treat me like a sex object?"

She smiled and shook her head. "How many glasses of wine did you drink tonight?"

"One."

"It certainly went to your head."

"No. Something else has gone to my head." His eyes caressed her as he leaned out of the sofa and pulled her onto his lap. "Now, what are those fantasies?"

She kissed him lightly. "I'd rather show than tell." This time it was his lips that covered hers and the kiss that ensued became deeper and more urgent. She tasted his need for her and felt a corresponding one for him growing within. Images whirled in her mind —a picture of her bandaging his arm, of him helping her down the steep slope, of her watching his mouth relax into a grin. The final one, the one that remained

136

fixed, was of them exploring and joining together in the dark intimacy of his bedroom.

Eric eased her down on the sofa and began unbuttoning the top piece of her plum dress while he spread a blanket of kisses over her cheeks. She watched, delighting in his caresses and savoring the warm wetness of his mouth against her skin. He opened her blouse and quickly discovered the front clasp to her bra, laying her breasts bare. Hungrily his mouth closed over the tip of one while he caressed the other with his hand.

With a sigh her eyes fluttered closed. His kisses went on and on, long and seductive on her breast, sweet and satisfying on her taut stomach and around her navel. She ruffled her fingers though his hair and down his shoulders, delighting in the transition from his downy hair to his tense, muscular shoulders.

Then he was pushing her skirt off and lifting her hips toward him, still blazing a torrent of kisses on her abdomen. Sensations that she couldn't name swirled through her as he drew her closer to him, his lips playing more gently on her. She felt fathomless desire and aching need and a sense of awe that a touch, a kiss, could bring her body so completely alive.

The only thing that was real, completely real, was his touch on one quivering part of her body. Her whole world was centered there. Even the strong hands holding her didn't quite seem tangible. And her hands gripping his shoulders weren't quite her own. Slowly, seductively, Eric touched and teased in a way that sent a jet of molten fire simmering along her veins. He drew her even closer against him and she felt herself slipping out of control until pleasure rolled over her in ever greater, ever more exquisite waves. Each built on the previous one, pounding through her before the first had subsided until they were coming so rapidly, so powerfully, there was no distinction between them and her body was consumed in one long, intense burst of joy.

When he released her hips, she sank weakly onto the sofa and Eric kissed her navel and breasts before stretching out beside her. Coiling her arms around his neck, she wrapped herself close to him and felt herself gliding toward sleep.

"Hey." He shook her gently. "You're not going to sleep, are you?"

"Mmmm." She nestled closer against him. He made a nice bed, not soft but warm.

Jacinda heard him chuckle softly and rise. Then he swept her into his arms, carried her into the bedroom, and laid her down. She wanted to sink blissfully into sleep in his arms, but he kept disturbing her—running his hands up and down her inner thighs, stroking her breasts in a sensuous pattern, and nibbling at her ear. Unconsciously she arched closer against him and he chuckled again.

Jacinda emerged from the blur of sleepiness into the cocoon of desire and began to explore his body as boldly as he had touched hers, kissing his flat nipples until they extended in pleasure, then running her hands down his waist and teasing at his thighs. Their mouths joined in a quest for fulfillment and they rolled sensuously over in the bed. First she was on top, feeling his lean body beneath her and moving hers in deliberately intoxicating ways and then he was above her again, pouring down hot kisses on her lips while his hands made erotic patterns on her bare thighs.

Then his body blended perfectly into hers and for a moment they both lay silent, savoring the ultimate closeness. Light shafted in from an opening in the curtains and she could see him looking down at her, a tender aggressor—one who wanted much but was willing to give much. She lifted her lips to him and his mouth singed hers as they began to move together.

Deftly they anticipated each other's movements in an erotic dance that spun ever faster. Yet every time she thought she would reach the summit, he shifted slightly and showed her another level of excitement, an unexplored sensation. Dazed with bliss, she reflected that the journey was almost as enjoyable as the end. Almost. But when she felt that churning, all-encompassing ecstasy, all else paled beside it. Then slowly she drifted downward again.

Giving him a final soft kiss, she curled against him, feeling his breath stir through her hair. She was no longer tired. Suddenly she wanted to talk, wanted to tell him about the magic that his lovemaking was to her.

"Eric?"

"Yes?"

She tried to think of a way to explain how she had felt, but words fell short. "When you touch me, it feels so . . ." She was going to say wonderful, but that wasn't strong enough. It didn't say nearly what she wanted to convey. Propping herself up on one elbow, she leaned toward him intently. "Have you ever heard of flashover? It happens during a fire."

"I don't guess I have." He put his hands casually behind his head and watched her with unconcealed amusement. "Somehow I thought right now your mind would be on other things besides the mechanics of a fire."

She continued slowly, almost thinking aloud. "When a room is on fire, it reaches a certain point of heat and then—in an instant—the whole room explodes in flames. That's what it feels like when you make love to me. The heat, the pleasure, reaches a certain point, and then it consumes me all at once."

He drew her back against him. "You may talk funny, but I like what you say."

Smiling, she ran her hands over the wiry hair on his chest. No other man had ever made her feel so complete. If only they were more alike, theirs could have been a romance with a happy ending. Yet they were holding each other now and that was all that was important. Smiling at that thought, she slipped into sleep.

It seemed like only a short time later when Jacinda awoke at the sound of Eric sliding out of bed and reaching for his clothes in the dark room.

"Where are you going?" she mumbled.

"Go back to sleep. Sorry I woke you."

She sat up in bed. He seemed to always be leaving her in the mornings and she hated it. "I'm awake now," she insisted. "Where are you going?"

"My parents are out of town and I've got to take care of their livestock. Then I have to go to the quarry."

"But it's Saturday," she objected.

"I know."

He made no promises about returning. She tossed back the covers. "I'm going with you."

He paused. "What?"

"I can help you."

"Oh, you can milk a cow, can you?"

Jacinda could hear his smile in the dusky room. "No, but I've seen you type, remember. I can definitely give you a hand at the office."

He came up beside her and drew her against him. "Yeah, my typing's cost me my last eight jobs," he agreed as he kissed her. "Mmm, I like kissing you early in the morning. It makes me feel like the rest of the day will go okay."

His kisses affected her the same way, especially after having been without them for so long. And she knew that the rest of the day would be perfect if she was close enough to him to fortify herself with his touch now and then. She dressed in jeans and a muslin peasant blouse and ten minutes later they were on the road. The sun was just rising.

"I saw Buford the other day," he said. "He's already run into a fence post and put a harelip on the truck." Eric shook his head. "Buford always did drive like a maniac."

"Everyone in New York drives like that," Jacinda observed lazily.

"Must be a terrible place. I can't see why anyone in their right mind would live there." His brown eyes danced with amusement.

"Just drive," she directed archly.

Eric's parents' house was within half a mile of his own. Acres of rolling farmland were surrounded by a fringe of woods. After pulling into the barnyard behind his parents' house, he parked near a long, low building.

"This is the hen house."

She trailed after him into the dim interior where she was greeted by a chorus of hundreds of squawking chickens. She halted uncertainly while those near the door leaped from their roosts and fled in terror.

"They're jumpy because they don't know us," Eric explained. "I'll get the feed while you start collecting the eggs." Picking up a bucket, he handed it to her. "Put them in here."

Jacinda had never collected eggs before. In fact,

she'd never even been inside a hen house and she wasn't at all sure that the chickens wouldn't attack her. Sweeping a glance around, however, she realized they seemed more wary of her than she was of them. Cautiously she stepped farther into the building and looked around. Where were the eggs anyway? she wondered, studying the straw beneath the row of roosts. She didn't see any eggs on the ground.

As she moved into the midst of the building, flustered chickens scattered before her. She stopped beside a row of boxes tilted on their sides and peered into one. Straw lined the bottom and in the center lay two eggs.

Gingerly she picked them up and put them in the bottom of the paper-lined bucket. Then she went to the next box. Collecting eggs was easy, she soon decided, and was feeling quite proud of her farm-girl prowess when she reached a nest with a chicken inside. Clucking ominously, it ruffled its feathers and eyed her malevolently.

Eric came up beside her. "Just stick your hand underneath her," he advised nonchalantly.

She stared at him. "Are you crazy?"

For an answer he reached under the hen and withdrew three eggs in one swift movement. The chicken looked at the empty nest and cackled piteously. "I'm going to start milking the cows. Come to the barn when you get finished here."

With a bemused shake of her head she went on to the next nest. Ten minutes later she'd filled the bucket with eggs as well as filling the soles of her shoes with a less desirable commodity. Eric smiled approvingly when she entered the barn.

"Come on, let's go finish milking the cows," he said.

"I'll observe, thanks. Tackling the chickens was enough for me for one day."

Jacinda watched while Eric sat down on a low stool beside a brown and white cow and began to milk. Up close the cows looked very big, much bigger than she had expected, and she kept a polite distance from them. "Did you do this when you were growing up?" she asked curiously.

"Of course." His smile seemed to say, Didn't everyone?

From the bale of hay where she sat, she drew a piece of straw out, still watching Eric's fingers move deftly. Her first impression of Eric would have blended well with the sight of him milking a cow. Since that first meeting, however, she had come to see him as a more complex person, one who was a mechanically gifted inventor, a nature enthusiast, and a sensitive lover. To learn that he was also at home in a barn seemed to add yet another dimension to him.

Rising, Eric picked up the stool. "Ready?"

"Yes."

"Watch your step," he cautioned.

After he had put the milk and eggs away, they returned to his car and he started down the lane. At its intersection with the main road, he turned left, the opposite direction from the quarry.

She looked around curiously. "Is this the right way to the quarry?"

"No, but I've decided my work can wait. I want to spend the day with you." He smiled at her before taking another turn down an unfamiliar road.

She smiled back. She liked the easy intimacy of his tone. "Where are we going?"

"I'm taking you to Arkansas's answer to Sotheby's." He grinned. "Ever been to an auction?"

"No."

"You'll enjoy it." Swinging the car around a wide curve, he drove over a rickety bridge and turned into a narrow lane. There he parked behind a line of cars stretching down from a white clapboard house.

The auction was already in progress when they reached the house. They made their way around to a backyard packed with people, furniture waiting to be sold, rusting milk cans, blue canning jars, and a thousand other household and farm items.

"Old Mrs. Reinhart lived here," Eric explained in a whisper that tickled deliciously at her ear. "She was almost a hundred when she died."

They edged in to the back of the crowd. On a makeshift platform an auctioneer in overalls was prattling a blue streak and patting a dilapidated rocking chair that listed dangerously to one side. "Genuine rocking chair. They don't make 'em like this anymore."

"Good thing too," someone at the front hollered.

"Did I hear two? Two dollars, Igottwo, now gimme three, three dollars, who'llgimmethree . . ." He was off and running in a racing, lilting blur of words that set hands motioning all over the yard. By the time he was through, he had sold the chair for one hundred and fifty dollars.

"I can't believe it," Jacinda whispered. As another item was set up for bids, she began to look around at the people. She recognized a couple of faces from the carnival, yet even the people she didn't know seemed somehow familiar. The older men and women looked stoic in a way that she had come to recognize as typically Arkansasan, while the younger people looked determined and hopeful. She smiled at the sight of a weathered old man whittling as he leaned against an equally weathered building.

Turning her attention back to the front, she saw the stack of merchandise waiting to be auctioned. A beautiful beveled glass mirror caught her attention. Nudging Eric, she pointed to it. "I like that mirror."

"Nice," he agreed.

"And that old trunk beside it. See it?" She indicated a wooden trunk with a bowed top. "Isn't that dollhouse precious too?"

"Sold to the lady in the back," the auctioneer concluded his furious rattle.

Eric clapped his hand around her shoulder. "Congratulations." Laughter danced in his brown eyes.

She looked at him blankly. "What?"

"You just bought that stuffed toy."

"I didn't buy anything!"

He chuckled. "Oh, yes, you did. Every time you pointed to something that you liked, the auctioneer was taking your bid."

"But I wasn't bidding!"

"I'm afraid you were. And quite a buy you got," he added heartily. "A stuffed possum that looks like it's as old as I am and a tad motheaten."

Her gray eyes were heavy with reproof. "You should have told me he was taking bids from me."

He was totally unrepentant.

Lifting her chin proudly, she looked away from him. But curiosity finally got the best of her and she leaned over to ask, "How much did I pay?"

"Thirty-five dollars."

Jacinda stared at him indignantly. "You let me pay thirty-five dollars for a beat-up old toy?"

His eyes widened innocently. "I thought you wanted it."

"Wait until we get off by ourselves," she warned.

"I'm looking forward to it." He smiled silkily.

CHAPTER TEN

Jacinda would have been more than content to spend the whole weekend with Eric. As luck would have it, however, she had already made plans for Sunday afternoon. Since Masie was convinced Jacinda wasn't meeting enough local people, she had invited her to attend a meeting of her sewing circle.

"But I can barely thread a needle," Jacinda had protested.

Masie laughed. "Honey, these girls aren't serious about sewing. They just want to get out of the house for a while so they join a stitch-and-bitch group. You'll have fun."

She would have had a lot more fun with Eric, Jacinda reflected when Masie picked her up after lunch on Sunday. She was wearing a middy blouse but at the last minute had exchanged the blue serge bloomers for navy slacks. She hadn't yet seen anyone wearing bloomers in Arkansas.

"Carrie doesn't live far from here," Masie said as she drove the station wagon down a winding street.

"How many women will be there?"

"Ten or so. I hope Ellen Parker doesn't come. She isn't speaking to Jane Thorton, which makes it very unpleasant. Here we are." Masie parked in front of a two-story brick house. "Last year Regina and Alice were on the outs for a while and Regina stabbed Alice's finger with a huge needle."

"On purpose?" Jacinda asked incredulously.

"Regina says it was an accident." They walked up a sidewalk bordered with yellow chrysanthemums.

"Point out Regina," Jacinda mumbled as Masie rang the bell. "I don't want to sit next to her."

A tall, raw-boned woman opened the door.

"Hello, Carrie," Masie said cheerfully, leading Jacinda into the living room where women ranging from their twenties to their sixties were seated around a quilting frame stretched out to the size of a double bed. After introductions were made, Masie took a chair in a corner. Jacinda was directed to a space between Ellen Parker and Jane Thorton.

Carrie handed her a threaded needle. "We're glad you could come. Ellen and Jane will help you get started."

"It's very easy, dear," Ellen said. "The lines for the pattern are drawn in pencil. Just follow them with stitches."

Jacinda carefully inserted the needle into the pure white cloth and brought it up to form one stitch. After comparing it with the row of stitches Ellen was forming, she decided it was perfect and made a second stitch.

Around the table the other women worked with nimble fingers, talking nonstop.

". . . he's been running around on her for years."

". . . I laid down the law to Jack. No husband of mine is going out to that place. You know what goes on there, don't you?"

Jacinda strained to hear what did go on, then realized with a start that her stitches had become long loops. The harder she concentrated on making them small and even, the worse they seemed to become. Self-consciously she looked around and saw Carrie watching her.

The tall woman pushed back her chair and rose. "Why don't you help me fix the tea, dear?" she suggested gently. "We've got all the hands we need sewing."

Gratefully Jacinda followed Carrie into the narrow kitchen, poured tea into glasses, and was carrying a tray back to the living room when she heard the others talking.

"She's dating Eric Fortner? I thought he was seeing Laura Kelly?"

Shamelessly Jacinda stopped to listen.

"Goodness no! That's all over."

"What happened?"

"I think Laura wanted to get married and Eric didn't."

"Shhh. She'll be back in a minute."

Everyone smiled blandly as Jacinda stepped into the living room. She smiled back, but she wished the women had continued their conversation about Eric.

Now that her ineptness at sewing had been established, she could enjoy the real entertainment of the afternoon—the gossip. Sitting on a sofa behind Marie, she watched the needles and tongues moving in time. She hadn't heard so much hometown gossip since *Peyton Place*.

Looking around the table, she smiled to herself. It was hard to believe how out of place she had felt when she arrived in Fayetteville. Right now, she felt very much at ease.

The next week passed in a glorious blur. Jacinda saw Eric often. She couldn't remember ever having felt so happy. She smiled when she sat at her desk; she smiled when she thought about Eric's nightly phone calls; she smiled just because she was alive. Sometimes, for no reason at all, she laughed aloud.

Saturday was an Indian summer day they spent flying a kite. When Eric scolded her for playing out the string wrong, she complained about his bossiness. Neither minded. They settled the dispute with a lingering kiss and the kite was forgotten as they returned to his house.

As soon as they were inside, he scooped her up and carried her into the bedroom. There he dropped her unceremoniously onto the bed, taking time to tickle her as he undressed her.

151

"Stop!" she panted, breathless with laughter as she tried vainly to capture his hands.

"No."

When he paused to undress, she attacked him. Although they wrestled playfully for several minutes, Jacinda was no match for him. Eric's body soon covered hers and he held her hands together over her head. All thoughts of escaping vanished as she felt the hard, lean lines of his body against her own bare flesh. And the relaxed, light-hearted mood between them affected her in a strange way, igniting a wild and hungry desire.

"Do you still want me to stop?" he asked as his hands began to move over her again. This time the playfulness was gone and his touch elicited startlingly sensual sensations.

"No," she breathed.

Her breasts felt swollen and tender as he caressed them. Her own hands slid down past the flat surface of his stomach to work their own magic. Then his mouth captured hers lazily, but his kisses gradually became more insistent. Jacinda felt tiny flames of desire lick through her as his tongue crept into her mouth. When he lowered his mouth to the taut tip of her breast, a delicious liquid warmth rolled through her.

She was swept into a gauzy world where Eric's pleasure was her pleasure and hers was his. She heard his every sharpened breath and felt each tensing muscle, and her own body responded with sensual instinct to his kisses and soft caresses. The moments spun out as they touched and kissed and felt desire building like waves being swept higher and higher by a coming storm. When they finally drew together, their physical union was merely an extension of their emotional bonding. He murmured a gentle endearment to her, and she stroked the curve of his back in reply. He brushed his lips against her ear and down her neck, and she arched closer to him, riding with him into the wild sea of passion. And even when she reached the pinnacle of ecstasy, she was not so lost in her own feeling that she didn't recognize Eric's own tumultuous response.

Afterward, she wound her arms around him and curled up near him to sleep, feeling sated and happy.

The next morning Jacinda awoke before Eric and lay for a long time watching him. He looked vulnerable and boyish in his sleep and that made her feel curiously protective of him. But she mustn't become too tender toward him, she warned herself. After all, they both knew this couldn't last. They were only going to take from each other what happiness they could until the spring. Then she would be gone.

But it was hard to think of leaving when Eric was lying there with his long lashes touching his cheek and his breathing a regular hum. With a soft smile she tucked the cover up closer around him and slid out of the bed. When she did, she knocked a book off the bedside table. She bent and picked up the thick volume, turning it over to read the title. *Lost Civiliza-*

tions. The subtitle explained that it was an "in-depth look at some of the great civilizations that have vanished from history."

"You awake?" he asked.

"Yes. Sorry I woke you."

"What are you doing on the floor?"

"I dropped something." She climbed back into bed, still holding the book. "Are you reading this?"

"I just finished it." He stifled a yawn. "Good book. I've read several by that author."

She studied him curiously. He had told her he read nonfiction, but she hadn't imagined that included books on archaeology. This was a new facet of Eric, and one that surprised her. "Are you interested in this sort of thing?"

"Sure."

"And you read a lot about ancient history?" she pressed, still trying to assimilate this new fact.

He shrugged. "Not just ancient history. I'm interested in all periods of history, but my favorite is medieval."

Jacinda could think of nothing to say. It seemed he was a man of constant surprises.

"Hungry?" he asked.

"Uh—yes." He handed her a robe and she pulled it on absently as he started from the room.

She wandered after him into the kitchen.

"Got any plans for lunch today?" he asked.

She leaned against him, stretching up on her toes

to rest her elbows on his shoulders and nibble at his ear. "I was hoping you'd feed me."

He grinned. "Not today. I'm going to my parents', but they'd love to have you come too."

"Are you sure?" she asked, knowing she wanted him to insist, so that they could spend the rest of the day together.

"Of course." He began putting bread into the toaster. "We'd better eat a light breakfast. Mom always cooks plenty in case a panzer division drops in. I'll call and let her know you're coming."

Four hours later Eric was introducing Jacinda to a petite woman with salt and pepper hair and warm brown eyes. "This is the one who so bravely collected the eggs," Eric informed his mother.

Mrs. Fortner gave her son a reproving look. "Don't pay any attention to him," she told Jacinda, putting her arm around her and drawing her into the living room.

His father rose from behind the paper and smiled at her. He was a big man with glasses perched on the end of his nose and a shock of white hair. "So you're the little girl from New York?" He looked toward his wife. "Pretty, isn't she, Mother?"

"Yes, she is."

Jacinda murmured a thank-you.

"But so thin," he continued as he surveyed her critically. "Don't you ever take the girl out to eat, son?"

"Occasionally."

Mr. Fortner turned back to Jacinda. "He'll have to take you out to eat more often. He's a good boy, my Eric is; he just needs to be reminded about these things."

Jacinda caught Eric's eye. He stood behind his parents, smiling wickedly.

"He's smart too," the older man added proudly.

"Yes, I know," Jacinda agreed.

"Did he ever tell you about the time he—"

Mrs. Fortner interrupted tactfully. "The food's ready. Why don't we go into the kitchen?"

They adjourned to the large country kitchen to eat at a table loaded with fried chicken, mashed potatoes, green beans, homemade bread, cole slaw, and Jell-O. Three pies waited on the sideboard.

Definitely not a meal for the fainthearted, Jacinda decided as Eric held her chair for her and she lifted the napkin from beside her plate.

"Have you lived in New York all your life, Jacinda?" Mrs. Fortner asked.

"Yes."

"Arkansas will seem like home in no time," Mr. Fortner assured her jovially.

"Jacinda is here only temporarily," Eric put in, looking at no one in particular. "In fact, she'll be going back in about three months."

His father raised his eyebrows. "Why do you want to go back to that big, noisy, dirty city?"

"Albert, that's her home," Mrs. Fortner chided gently.

"Yes, but the crime there is so terrible! Why would anyone want to live there when it's so safe here."

"The Harts were robbed just last month," Eric's mother reminded her husband and added with a smile toward Jacinda, "A lot of people love New York. They think it's the only civilized city in the world."

"Do they think that during the garbage strikes?" Mr. Fortner wanted to know.

His wife pursed her lips at him. "Don't pay any attention to him, dear," she advised Jacinda.

Beneath the table Eric caught her hand and pressed it. His smile and the look he telegraphed seemed to say, Yeah, he's a little contrary, but he's my dad and that's just the way he is. Jacinda smiled to herself, reflecting that if this conversation had been taking place at her own parents' table, she would be giving that same smile to Eric while her father wondered aloud how anyone could live in Arkansas.

Mrs. Fortner graciously steered the conversation into other waters while Mr. Fortner worried about Jacinda's slimness and pressed food on her. Eric's eyes professed his amusement at her plight. After dinner his mother took Jacinda out to see the baby chicks that had hatched two days ago. They were kept in a corner of the hen house caged off from the rest of the building.

"Can I pick them up?" Jacinda asked, carefully standing in the midst of a sea of chirping yellow fluff.

"Of course."

Scooping one up, she touched it gently. The fuzzy little ball cheeped mildly as it explored the palm of her hand. Jacinda stroked the downy yellow chick. "It's cute."

"I like chickens. They aren't smart, but they don't give me many problems either." Mrs. Fortner laughed. "Not like having a son who conducts chemistry experiments in my basement."

"Did Eric do that?" Jacinda asked curiously, and hoped Mrs. Fortner would divulge more.

"Oh, yes. With his father's blessing," she added dryly. "I nearly had a heart attack."

"Was it for a school project?"

"No. This was after he'd quit school. He was helping his father on the farm at the time and spending all of his nights in the basement. Eric's always been fascinated by finding out how things work," she added. "Ready to go?"

"Yes." Jacinda placed the chick back with its tiny fellows clustered around her feet and left the building with Mrs. Fortner. She was glad she'd come. Talking with Eric's parents was revealing much about him. He must have always had a great hunger for knowledge.

"Didn't he date?" Jacinda probed as they crossed the barnyard.

"Oh, yes. Weekends." Mrs. Fortner smiled reflectively. "And when he wasn't dating, he was usually thinking about girls. For a while a certain Betsy kept him too distracted to work. She was twice his age and built like a brick outhouse, as I believe the saying goes. She didn't know he was alive."

"She worshipped me," Eric contradicted from behind them.

"How long have you been back there eavesdropping?" The fondness of his mother's smile belied her reproach.

"Betsy?" Mr. Fortner mused beside Eric. "Was she that grass widow with a sway to her walk that could make you seasick?"

"Grass widow?" Jacinda asked.

"Divorcée," Eric interpreted. "And she adored me," he added as he put his arm around Jacinda. "I was in my prime then."

"You were sixteen," his mother said wryly.

The easygoing banter continued throughout the rest of the afternoon. Jacinda liked the atmosphere. The Fortners obviously enjoyed being with one another, and no one got mad even when they played cards and Mr. Fortner was caught cheating twice. He huffed indignantly and was allowed to keep his winnings of several toothpicks.

On the way back to Eric's house, Jacinda leaned over and kissed him. "Your parents are nice."

"Dad tends to be a little opinionated," he observed with a chuckle.

She laughed. "I've noticed that most fathers are. Mine is no exception."

"It's just that Dad has always lived in the country

159

and he can't believe you'll really go back to New York."

She slanted a glance at him. "Can you?"

"Of course."

Her immediate reaction was disappointment that he hadn't said he wished she would stay. But that was nonsense, she scolded herself. She should be glad Eric understood she wasn't here permanently. It would make everything much simpler when it came time to leave.

They drove the rest of the way to his house in companionable silence. Hand in hand, they walked into the bedroom and slipped out of their clothes.

Afterward, Jacinda leaned over to whisper in his ear. "From what I've seen, I don't believe sixteen was your prime."

When the phone rang the next evening, Jacinda picked it up quickly, hoping it was Eric. It was Philip.

"Got any plans for the weekend?"

She chewed her bottom lip uncertainly. Now that she was so involved with Eric, she knew that it was impossible to be anything but friends with Philip. "I think we need to talk, Philip," she said slowly.

After a moment's silence he laughed dryly. "No, I don't think we do. You've said it all by the tone of your voice. 'I like you very much as a friend but I don't think we could ever be more.' Am I right?"

"I'm sorry."

"It's okay." His jaunty tone fell flat. "Just out of curiosity, is there someone else?"

"Yes."

"Someone from Arkansas?"

"Yes."

Again he laughed dryly. "Well, it's your life, but somehow I can't imagine you stuck here in an outpost of civilization for the rest of your life. And even rustic charm pales after a while." Sighing heavily, he began again, "I'm sorry, Jacinda, I have no right to be sarcastic. You've been honest with me and you've never led me on. I appreciate that."

"Maybe we can get together sometime for a friendly game of chess." She didn't know what else to say.

"Maybe."

Both knew they never would.

"Well, tell old Jim Peters hi for me while you're home at Christmas," she said.

"I will."

She hung up and sat staring down at the phone. In the beginning she had been so convinced Philip was the perfect man for her. But the heart and the head didn't always see things the same way and it wasn't Philip who made her heartbeat flutter. It was Eric.

And Eric, she was discovering, wasn't the man she had originally believed him to be. He was much more complex than she had first thought. He read archaeology books, did experiments in his spare time, and had impressed a Stanford professor with his engineering accomplishments.

Jacinda was considering all of those facts the next day at work when Masie breezed into the office.

"Okay," the other woman said briskly, "I'm selling tickets to the Harvest Fair. How many do you want?"

"The what?"

"The Harvest Fair. It's two weeks from now. We have square dancing, a hayride—the works. Last year someone set the hay wagon on fire, but I can't promise anything that exciting this year."

A smile curved Jacinda's lips upward. A fire wouldn't be necessary. She and Eric could make their own excitement. "I'll buy two."

"Good girl." Masie tore the tickets from a booklet. "That'll be twenty dollars and well worth it."

Jacinda was opening her purse as Lann sauntered into the room. "Don't you read the signs, lady? No soliciting."

"Quiet. I'm in the middle of a sale." Masie accepted the money from Jacinda and handed her the tickets. "Are you going with Eric or Philip?" she fished.

"Tell her to mind her own business," Lann suggested laconically.

"Hush." Masie turned back to Jacinda. "Who did you say, dear?"

"Eric."

"Good! I was hoping you two would get together. He's such a nice man. Of course Philip is too," Masie added as an afterthought. "But he seemed a little standoffish."

162

"Come on, Masie, scoot on out of here and let my help get back to work." Putting an arm around his wife, he led her from the room.

Thoughtfully Jacinda watched them go. Yes, Philip was standoffish, just as she had been when she first arrived. In fact, *snob* probably wouldn't be too harsh a word. The first things she had noticed about the Arkansans were their accents and their clothes. Now she could look beyond that and see friendly, hard-working people.

She smiled as she realized just how much she was already looking forward to taking Eric to the Harvest Fair.

CHAPTER ELEVEN

Saturday Jacinda and Eric spent the day going to garage sales. Although it was November, it was one of those days that rightfully belonged to early September, with its mild winds and clear sun. After eating dinner at her house, they sat on the sofa, both feeling lazy and relaxed.

"I bought tickets for a thing called the Harvest Fair. It's next Saturday night." Drowsily she fingered the soft wool of his shirt. "Want to be my date?"

"I guess so. The other girls I asked out are all busy then." He idly picked up one of the pieces from the nearby chess set.

"Are you still playing?" she asked.

"Trying." He grinned ruefully. "I've taught myself from a book, but I've never played with anyone."

"You haven't!" Jacinda uncurled from the sofa and rose. "Let's fix that right now." She picked up the board and carried it to the kitchen table.

Eric didn't follow. "Maybe that's not a good idea."

"It's all right," she reassured him with a smile. "I know you're a beginner. I'll teach you."

Shrugging, he crossed to the table and casually rested his elbows on it.

"Now, then, the first thing you do is—"

He reached across the table and brushed back her hair. "You're cute when you're serious. You're not going to cream me, are you?"

"Of course not." She lifted his hand off her and kissed the palm of it before setting it firmly down on the table. "It's good strategy to distract your partner, but it won't work with me."

There was a teasing glint in his eyes. "What will work with you?"

Jacinda cleared her throat delicately. "As I was saying, the first move is—"

Abruptly, Eric rose, walked to the window, and stood with his back to her. "I don't think we should play."

"Why not?" She watched him curiously. For the past two weeks she'd seen a very carefree side of Eric. But he was serious now; she could tell by the straight set of his shoulders and the way he ran his fingers through his hair. Why didn't he want to play?

"You know how competitive some people get at games," he said. "We might both end up getting mad."

"Come over here and sit down," she directed with a smile. So that was it. He didn't want to lose to her. She was surprised that the thought of losing to her bothered him so much. As male egos went, Eric's was pretty laid back, and he didn't seem easily threatened.

But perhaps she had misjudged him on that point, too, she reflected. There seemed to be so many things about him that surprised her. She would win, of course, but she would let the game run awhile before she did.

"It's a friendly game," she encouraged, and added lightly, "I didn't know how to pick up eggs, but I was willing to learn. I've spent the last three months learning to do things that are new to me. Don't you think it's your turn?"

He sat down across from her. "Who goes first?"

The game started slowly. Eric made a surprisingly good move to guard his knight. When he took her first pawn, she praised him lavishly. When he took her second, she wasn't so lavish; she had yet to capture any of his men.

The game was over fifteen minutes later. Jacinda sat stunned. Beginner's luck, she told herself. How else could Eric have won when she was such a good chess player? Her spirit of competition charged to the fore. It was a little humiliating to lose to someone whom she'd offered to teach.

"Let's play again," she said briskly. He might have beat her once, but he certainly wouldn't win a second time. Her guard was up now, and she realized she had been too relaxed during the first game.

"Jacinda, I don't think we should," Eric said gently.

He thought he could beat her again! Well, he couldn't. "I think it's a great idea," she countered and began setting up the board again. This time there was no idle conversation between them. She sat tensely, waiting for him to move, and then countered each move brilliantly. This was more like it, she told herself as she narrowed in on his knight.

"Check," he said quietly.

She gasped. How had he done that? Belatedly she realized she had been watching his knight so closely that she had made a beginner's mistake. Still, she had to admit that Eric had made some darn good moves to put her in this position. She felt taken aback by his skill and her concentration was shattered.

Added to that, Eric looked calm and completely in control as he sat with one arm resting on the back of the chair. He didn't even deliberate long before his moves but seemed to take in the whole board at a glance, the brown eyes sweeping over the carved figures with cool appraisal. Behind those clear eyes, behind that casual air, she realized, was a man who could easily match wits with her. And that was an aspect of Eric that she had never considered before.

Rattled and defensive, she made a final rash move. He won. Wordlessly he began putting the set away.

"Well, you certainly learn quickly," she said with false cheer. Childish as it seemed Eric now felt like a threat. She didn't stop to sort out her tangled reasoning, but she did know it had something to do with the fact she had a master's in engineering while he had quit high school. Added to that, she had been playing chess for years while he was only a beginner.

"You're mad at me," Eric stated flatly. "I was afraid this would happen."

She was mad, even though she knew she had no reason to be. But she had been so sure she would win. Added to that, his calm acceptance of his victory stung. "Oh, so you knew all along you were going to win?" she challenged. "Just what made you think you could beat me?"

He lifted his shoulders and let them fall nonchalantly. "I catch on to most things pretty quickly. I thought I understood the game."

She slumped back in her chair, her anger already fading, trying to figure out why she'd been so upset. She had thought she knew Eric. Of course she had realized early on that he had a good aptitude for mechanical things, but she still hadn't thought he could compete with her.

She lifted her eyes to Eric, taking in the blond hair, the handsome face, the big hands. He looked the same as he had ten minutes ago; but he wasn't the same to her.

Restlessly she picked up one of the chess figures and toyed with it. She had been playing since she was thirteen, and she could beat most people she knew. But she hadn't beat Eric and she knew instinctively if they played a thousand rematches, he would win them all.

"For heaven's sake, it's only a game," he said impatiently.

Her thoughts were no longer on the game. She had underrated him. Even after he had proven her wrong about the conveyor and even after Dr. Metcalf had impressed on her what a remarkable achievement Eric had made, she had continued to see him as only mechanically gifted. But she could no longer ignore how truly intelligent he was. How else had she underestimated him?

Impatiently he pushed back his chair. "Do you want me to leave?"

"No!" She reached across the table and caught his arm. "I was being a sore loser, but I'm over that now."

He searched her face. "Sure?"

"Positive." She managed a smile. "However, you do turn your back on me at your own risk."

His smile dawned slowly. "I'll remember that." He scooped her up as effortlessly as if she were a child and carried her into the bedroom. "I'll make my formal apologies now."

They made love with a slow, burning intensity. For a few moments Jacinda managed to lose herself in her passion. But when they both subsided back onto the bed, her doubts returned. Suddenly she felt very unsure of herself. She had been wrong about so many things.

For the first time she wondered if she wasn't planning to leave a man who was exactly what she wanted. A month ago she had believed she could end their relationship once it was time to return to New York. Now she didn't know. . . .

The next day Jacinda was still plagued by her thoughts and had difficulty concentrating on her work. When the phone rang, she picked it up absently.

"Jacinda? Jim Peters here. I've got great news for you!"

"Oh?"

"We've hired a new man and he's willing to come to Arkansas to take your place. You can pack your bags right now."

She blinked in astonishment. Go back to New York? *Now?* Her lips moved but formed no words.

"Are you still there?" Jim asked.

"Yes," she managed shakily. "I'm still here."

"Good news, isn't it?" he said jovially. "Well, I won't keep you because I know you've got a million things to do. I've already talked to Lann and squared everything with him. This will be your last week there. Try to be back here by next Monday. 'Bye."

"Jim!"

"Yes?"

A feeling of panic was overtaking her first stunned reaction. "I—I wouldn't mind staying in Arkansas a little longer."

"No, I don't want you to do that. You've done your time. Besides, this man doesn't object and I've already put the paperwork through. See you." He hung up.

Very carefully Jacinda set the phone down. She felt disoriented, as if her life was slipping out of control. But one thing was certain; she didn't want to go home. Not now.

Lann appeared at her door a moment later. "Jim Peters call you?"

She nodded mutely.

The short, heavy man ambled into the room. "I hate to see you go. You were just starting to develop a nice twang." He chuckled at his own joke.

Jacinda couldn't dredge up a smile; she simply stared blankly. A week. She had only a week before she would be back in New York. She felt trapped and a little desperate.

"Something wrong?"

"No, nothing." At least there wouldn't be if she didn't burst into tears. But right now she felt perilously close to doing just that.

"Well, I just thought I'd make sure you knew."

She stared after him as he left. This couldn't have come at a worse time, she thought bleakly. And she was still too stunned to sort everything out.

From the time she had started dating Eric, it had been understood their relationship would be a temporary one. Only that had been then. This was now. And right now she didn't think she could leave him.

But how did Eric feel? She thought he felt as strongly for her as she did for him, but her judgments about Eric had been wrong so often, she couldn't be sure. It was frightening to consider offering herself to him only to be rejected. What if he didn't want a permanent relationship?

Agitated, she prowled around her office, her work entirely forgotten. At noon she walked around downtown with her head bent and her brows furrowed.

The thought of leaving was wrenching. She wanted to stay with Eric. But now the one problem that she had never considered before stared her in the face. Did he want her to stay? Oh, sure, they had had fun together, but they had begun their relationship with the understanding it was temporary. Had that been what he wanted?

Miserably, she remembered that only last weekend he had told her he understood she would return to New York. And he'd sounded casual and unperturbed Sunday when he had told his mother she would be leaving in the spring. Plus there were those whispered comments about Laura at the sewing party. *Laura had wanted marriage and he hadn't.*

With a sigh Jacinda pushed back the wisps of hair blowing across her face. The truth of the matter was she didn't know what Eric wanted. And the only way to find out was to present the facts to him. But she wouldn't push herself on him. She would let him know how much he meant to her, but she wouldn't

172

insist on staying. If he wanted her to, he would tell her so. And she prayed that he would.

At five o'clock she left the office and drove directly to Eric's house. After parking behind his car, she drew in a steadying breath, walked to the door, and knocked.

Eric opened the door a moment later and smiled at her. "I didn't know you were coming out tonight. Come in." He put his arm around her and ushered her into the living room. "Sit down."

They sat side by side on the sofa. Although she had carefully rehearsed what she was going to say, now that she was here, the words came tumbling out. "I had a phone call from my boss in New York today. I'm going back there at the end of this week."

His expression became guarded. After a long silence he asked, "For good?"

She nodded wordlessly.

"Well, I guess you're pleased about that." Standing, he sunk his hands into his pockets and walked to the window.

She rose, crossed to him, and put her arms around him. The tears were sliding down her cheeks now, blurring her vision. "Hold me," she whispered, and he did. But it wasn't like the other times he had held her. This time she could feel the reserve, as if he were already drawing away from her. Surely he would beg with her not to go! She clutched even tighter, feeling she held her heart in her hand as she waited for him to speak.

Gently he removed her hands and walked away. "This is rather sudden, isn't it?"

"Th-they found someone to replace me here." She willed him to turn toward her, but he didn't. He simply stood with his back to her, hands thrust into pockets and head tilted up as if he were studying the ceiling. The silence lengthened.

A knot began to form in her throat as she waited. She had told him she was leaving and he hadn't asked her to remain. In fact, he was letting her go without even a protest, as if he had been prepared to release her all along.

The thought of leaving Eric had been painful, but the fact that he didn't seem to care was even more devastating. Had her appeal for him from the beginning been the fact they could only have a short-term relationship? Hurt and incomprehension and betrayal swirled in her mind. She had thought he cared so much!

When he finally turned toward her, a slight smile played on his lips. "I'm sorry it's ending so soon. We had some good times, didn't we?"

She felt chilled. Eric wasn't going to say the only thing she wanted to hear. He wasn't going to say he loved her or plead with her to stay. Looking at him now, it was hard to believe this man had ever held her and made love to her. He seemed like a stranger. And his words were courteous and detached—the sort of thing you might say to a casual acquaintance you'd never see again. Suddenly she had to get away.

"Well, I'd better get back to my apartment." She wanted to sound cheerful, but heard the strain in her voice. "I have a million things to do."

"I'm sure you do."

There seemed nothing more to say. They stared at each other for a moment, then she picked up her coat and left. It was the first time Jacinda had been on these desolate roads alone at night, but she didn't even think about that. She was far more aware of the desolation within. Eric hadn't even followed her to the door. Her bottom lip quivered as she rounded a curve.

It was a long, tear-stained night. Even the extra blusher and careful makeup she applied the next morning didn't succeed in covering the hollows under her eyes. Without knowing how she managed it, she got through the next few days. Every night she waited for Eric to call and tell her it had all been a terrible mistake. But he didn't.

That weekend she packed her things and flew back to New York.

CHAPTER TWELVE

Three days after Jacinda left, Eric mailed his paper to Dr. Metcalf. Now there was nothing to do but wait for the professor's comments. He almost wished he had kept it longer. He'd started it when Jacinda had told him she was going—at least while he was working on it, he had been able to shove thoughts of Jacinda to the back of his mind. Most of the time. But at night when he lay in that empty bed, it was impossible not to think about her.

He'd been stunned when she told him she was leaving, and he'd waited for her to say she didn't want to go. But she hadn't said that. Why would she? She had wanted to go. It was what she had longed for from the minute she reached Arkansas. Only he had been foolish enough to believe that given a little time, he might be able to change her mind. But he hadn't had enough time. Who knew? Maybe all the time in the world wouldn't have been enough.

In the beginning he had been merely intrigued by Jacinda. She had seemed so stiff and aloof in that grand office of hers that he had wanted to explore further. But his attraction had soon grown beyond anything he could control.

Thank God he hadn't embarrassed both of them by pleading with her to stay. She had no choice but to go, just as he had to remain here. This was where his work was; New York was where hers was. It was that simple.

How he had wanted to stop her! At least he had been able to be gallant and civilized until she left. And she would never have to know that he had smashed his fist against a wall two minutes after she walked out the door.

It was snowing when the plane touched down in New York. Her sister, Liz, met her at the airport. After greeting her with a warm hug, Liz looked her over. "You seem pretty much the same to me. Everyone here's been taking bets on whether or not you'd come back wearing a homespun dress and sunbonnet."

Jacinda smiled wanly. "No, I left those behind in Arkansas." Along with a few other things she wished desperately she still had.

"I'm glad you're back. Come on, let's get your things and get out of here."

Jacinda followed slowly. LaGuardia looked like a remake of *The Snake Pit*. Dazed people waited for flights that had been delayed yet another time. Women with screaming children jostled with passengers carrying bulging shopping bags. Tempers were short and shins were damaged. Jacinda felt tired and defeated as she struggled through the airport, shrugging past a bald, berobed man who tried to convert her to a Middle Eastern religion.

Liz sailed along, unperturbed by the crowds. In fact, she seemed not to notice them at all, but Jacinda felt completely hemmed in and kept falling behind her sister and stopping to apologize when she bumped into someone.

"Are you coming?" Liz threw over her shoulder.

"Yes." Jacinda hurried to catch up. Once they had picked up her luggage they crossed to the parking lot and located Liz's car. While her sister swerved out into the maze of traffic, Jacinda collapsed in the seat beside her. "Thanks for coming to meet me."

Liz threw her a smile. "Glad to be back?"

"Of course," she lied. It was lousy to be back. She felt even worse here than she had during that last miserable week in Arkansas. At least there she had clung to the hope Eric would call. Now that possibility went from remote to nonexistent.

Forty-five minutes later they reached her apartment building and she and Liz carried the suitcases up to the sixth floor. Liz set a suitcase inside the apartment door and studied her. "You haven't said two words since we left the airport. Are you depressed or just tired?"

"Both."

"Want to talk about it?"

178

Jacinda sank onto the sofa. "I'm afraid I'll start crying if I do."

"Uh-oh, that bad, huh? I take it we're talking about that man you were dating in Arkansas?"

"Eric." It was a name that had gone around in her head a thousand times this past week. But this was the first time she had said it aloud since she had spoken with him. It hung in the air as a presence in its own right.

"What happened?" Liz asked sympathetically.

Her lips trembled, but she tried to sound casual. "When I told him I was leaving he said, 'It's been nice knowing you,' or words to that effect."

Her sister tilted her head to one side. "What did you want him to say?"

Her throat felt even thicker. "I don't know. I was kind of hoping he'd throw himself in front of the plane so I couldn't leave."

"You wanted to stay in Arkansas?" Liz asked incredulously. "I thought you were dying to get back to New York?"

"I thought I was too," Jacinda murmured. "I thought a lot of things that turned out to be wrong." She continued slowly, as if speaking to herself. "It's funny, but in the beginning I had all these reasons why Eric was all wrong for me. I didn't think he was educated or polished enough and I was sure my attraction for him was purely physical. I couldn't have been more wrong."

"Poor kid." Liz patted her shoulder. "Listen, I've

179

got to run; I'm parked illegally, but I'll see you at Mom and Dad's tonight for dinner and we'll talk. Okay?"

"Yeah. Thanks for picking me up." After Liz left, Jacinda stood looking around her apartment. The street noises sounded like distant melodies and she remembered how she had pined for them during those first nights in Arkansas. Now she was equally at home amid silence. Only, of course, here there would be no silence; there would always be the city sounds to keep her company.

Mechanically she carried her suitcases into the bedroom and began to unpack, turning the radio up loud to distract herself with music. It didn't work. With every outfit she unfolded, she recalled details of when and where she had worn it with Eric.

"I'm not going to cry," she told herself aloud. But it was so hard not to when her throat ached from holding back the tears.

Resolutely she dug into the suitcase again and her hands closed around a soft, furry object. "Oh, God," she whispered and sank down on the bed clutching the motheaten old toy possum. Who would cry over a stupid, deteriorating piece of junk? But she couldn't help herself. It brought back memories of the auction.

And that memory unleashed a flood of others. She thought about their trek into the cave with its gleaming crystal walls, about the carnival when he had first kissed her, about the night at his house when she had bandaged his raw arm. It wasn't going to be easy forgetting Eric. But she was going to have to try.

The days crawled by. Jacinda had trouble sleeping nights and she knew her work was suffering from her inability to concentrate.

At the end of the week she was lying awake at three in the morning when the doorbell sounded. Tossing her robe over her shoulders, she moved cautiously toward the door. "Who is it?" she called as she squinted through the peephole.

"Eric."

Her heart thumping, she threw the door open and stared incredulously. "Eric?" she whispered in disbelief.

He had a suitcase under one arm and an overcoat under the other. Slowly he set the suitcase on the floor and laid the coat on top of it. Then he rose to face her. "I had a speech all made up, Jacinda. It sounded real pretty, but I can't remember it. All I know is that I've been miserable without you."

She blinked dazedly.

"We can work something out, can't we?" His face showed finely etched lines of strain. "If you don't want to come back to Arkansas, then I'll move to New York. Only don't say it's over."

She shook her head, slowly at first, then faster. "It isn't over!"

They both reached to touch each other at the same moment—tentatively, shyly, as if each feared the

181

other would vanish. Jacinda stroked her fingers over his face and felt the smooth planes of it and the warmth of his breath as her fingertips trailed over his lips. Then she tumbled into his arms and he engulfed her in a fierce hug. "Oh, Eric," she whispered.

Their kiss was searching, intense, and bittersweet. Finally she tore herself away from him. "I was so wrong about you—about us—about everything." She wanted to explain everything to him but couldn't find the words.

Upstairs someone opened a door and called down, "Hey, I'm trying to sleep."

Eric glanced up, then looked back at her with a smile. "I'd like to stay here tonight if that's all right with you." The endearingly familiar dimple appeared. "If not, I've already met a nice woman who invited me back to her place."

She dragged him into her apartment. "I'll nail the door shut if you try to leave."

Then they were in each other's arms again and their mouths clung in fevered need. She held him tightly, as if by loosening her grip she would lose him again.

After endless moments he drew back. "I've missed you," he said unevenly.

"I've missed you too. Terribly," she added fervently and buried her face against his chest.

He touched her hair. "Then why have we both spent the last week being miserable?"

"Because you didn't ask me to stay!" She pounded

on his chest, not from anger but from a need to release the turbulent emotions. "Why didn't you stop me from leaving?"

He trapped her hands beneath his. "Because I thought you wanted to go." He smiled. "I was being noble. That lasted a full week, then I decided to hell with nobility. I didn't like the way it felt."

"But I didn't know you wanted me to stay!"

He chuckled and touched her cheek. "We can iron all this out later. It's late and I'm tired. Do you have an extra bed?"

"No."

"Good."

When he reached for his suitcase, she saw the tag. "You took the bus?" she asked incredulously. "You took the bus all the way from Arkansas? Why?"

"I don't like trains," he answered simply.

"I can see we still have a lot of work to do to make a city slicker out of you. When we go back to Arkansas, we're flying."

He looked up quickly. "Are we going back? The traffic here scares the hell out of me, but I'll get used to it if you'd rather stay. On the other hand, if we went back, we could come to New York for plays and operas whenever you like. And the Met comes to Dallas once a year—I've checked. And we could go to Kansas City to the symphony."

"I'll have to talk to Jim Peters, but I'm pretty sure I could get a permanent job in Fayetteville." She giggled, feeling light-hearted and unable to control her joy. "The bad thing is it's too late to use those tickets to the Harvest Fair."

He drew her hands down to her side and kissed her gently. "Have I told you that I love you?"

"Prove it," she whispered with a catch in her voice.

He led her down the hall, making two wrong stops at the closet and bathroom doors before he located the bedroom.

He turned the light on and began undressing her reverently while she helped him remove his own clothes. They came together with a passion that had been heightened by their separation. Desperately hungry for each other, they touched and explored urgently, as if to make up for lost time. The physical release of their pent-up need was wild and sweet. Afterward, Jacinda lay beside him running her hands over his chest.

She had never felt such deep contentment before. Each time they had made love before, no matter how breathtakingly passionate the moment had been, she had known that it was not to last. Only now she knew that it could last. Forever.

He tweaked back a curl. "What are you thinking?"

"That we're going to have the rest of our lives together, and I think I'm going to like that." She leaned over to plant a dewy kiss on his chest.

"You will," he murmured. "I'll see to it that you do."

Slipping his hand under her chin, he turned her

face up to his. For a moment that spun out endlessly, they simply gazed at each other. Thoughts of love ran through Jacinda's mind, and she could read them in Eric's eyes as well. But the feelings were too deep, too special, for words to adequately express. They drew closer and his mouth moved gently over hers.

She responded with an answering kiss, and then she was tucked securely against his body again while their kisses spiraled into more passionately intimate exchanges. She slid her hands over the smoothly planed muscles of his back and down to his thighs and felt his dormant desire reawaken.

"Do you know how many times I've dreamed of holding you like this since you left?" he whispered against her ear.

The feel of his breath stirring on the sensitive lobe of her ear sent delicious shivers down her spine. "Not as many times as I dreamed of holding you like this." She ended her words with a kiss that drew them both deeper into the cocoon of mutual need.

The urgency of their first lovemaking had been replaced with a glorious calmness that came from the serenity of knowing they had all the time in the world. Their kisses were languid and their touches gentle strokes. Jacinda let her hands slide over his body and felt his hands moving over her in a way that aroused, yet satisfied. The intensity of their passion built gradually, until their bodies slipped together with the effortlessness of love and familiarity. Their kisses became more intimate and demanding and hands explored with greater need.

Wrapped in a gauzy fog, Jacinda felt Eric's pleasure become her own. His moans of pleasure excited her and it was sheer bliss to feel the response in his body to her sighs. They rocked together with growing momentum until the first embers of ecstasy blazed into a blinding, consuming light. This time when that blossom of pure sensation deep within her unfolded, she clutched him tighter to her, needing to feel his emotions as deeply as she felt her own. And when she subsided back onto the bed, Jacinda realized she hadn't experienced this lovemaking in terms of *her* response, but as *their* response. And that made her radiant with happiness.

Eric pulled her atop his damp body and tucked back her hair. "Why are you smiling?" he asked with hoarse tenderness.

"Because just now when we made love I felt that I was completely one with you. I like that." She dipped her head to kiss the tip of his nose.

"Then we'll make love often," he offered gallantly.

"Good." She was suddenly serious. What if Eric hadn't come to New York and they had never gotten together? It was a thought that frightened her, for she now saw clearly all that she would have missed and how empty her life would have been without him. Burying her head against his bare shoulder, she wrapped her arms fiercely around him.

"Oh, Eric, it took me so long to realize a lot of

things about you. From the very beginning, I was narrow-minded and—"

He stopped her words with a kiss. "Hey, I'm not going to listen to you saying unkind things about my future wife."

She laughed softly and moved closer to him. "I wouldn't dare argue with my future husband."

Candlelight

Ecstasy Romances™

$1.95 each

$2.50 each